CAL

D0999707

5

J
Wesl   Wesley, Mary

Speaking terms

110995

Calloway County Public Library
710 Main Street
Murray, KY 42071

1. Books may be kept two weeks and may be renewed once for the same period, except 7 day books and magazines.

2. A fine is charged for each day a book is not returned according to the above rule. No book will be issued to any person incurring such a fine until it has been paid.

3. All injuries to books beyond reasonable wear and all losses shall be made good to the satisfaction of the Librarian.

4. Each borrower is held responsible for all books charged on his card and for all fines accruing on the same.

Speaking Terms

Other Mary Wesley titles published
by The Overlook Press

Haphazard House
The Sixth Seal

Speaking Terms
Mary Wesley

THE OVERLOOK PRESS
WOODSTOCK · NEW YORK

First published in The United States in 1994 by
The Overlook Press
Lewis Hollow Road
Woodstock, New York 12498

Copyright © 1969 Mary Wesley

All Rights Reserved. No part of this publication may be reproduced or transmitted
in any form or by any means, electronic or mechanical, including photocopy,
recording, or any information storage and retrieval system now known or to be
invented without permission in writing from the publisher, except by a reviewer
who wishes to quote brief passages in connection with a review written for
inclusion in a magazine, newspaper, or broadcast.

Library of Congress Cataloging-in-Publication Data

Wesley, Mary
Speaking terms / Mary Wesley.
p. cm.
Summary: A group of English children use their newly found ability
to speak to animals in order to protect wild creatures.
[1. Animals–Fiction. 2. Human-animal communication–Fiction.
3. England–Fiction.] I. Title.
PZ7.W5Sp 1994
[Fic]–dc20
94-1525
CIP
AC
Originally published in Great Britain by J.M. Dent,
a division of the Orion Publishing Group.

ISBN: 0-87951-524-4
135798642

First Edition

To Phyllis Jones

My elder sister Angela gave me a bullfinch in a cage for my birthday, before the laws were made to prevent people keeping beautiful wild birds in cages. The bullfinch was very wild, not unnaturally as he had been limed and his feet never really recovered from their injuries.

I loved him. I loved his fat pink stomach. I loved his black head. I loved his large wholly brown eyes.

Years passed and my bullfinch grew quite happy and contented in his cage. He flew about the room and made little piping noises. He puffed himself up round with affection when I came near him and he piped when he heard the wild birds outside in the garden.

'It is cruel,' I said to myself, 'to keep such a beautiful bird in captivity. He should at least have some freedom.'

For a long time I thought about this because Mr Bull, as I called him, had become part of my life and I did not wish to lose him.

One morning I cleaned his cage and fed him, giving him more hempseed than usual. Hempseed is not really good for bullfinches but they love it.

'Mr Bull, shall I ever see you again?' I asked, but he just looked at me with his enormous brown eyes and said nothing.

'Mr Bull, I'm going to give you a treat,' I said.

I carried him downstairs in the early morning and out into the garden. An almond tree was coming into flower. Its buds showed pink and my father was greatly looking forward to the full glory of the tree.

I opened the door of Mr Bull's cage and waited. Mr Bull, very fat, came and sat by the open door.

'Go on, Mr Bull,' I said. 'You can fly.'

Mr Bull spread his wings and flew into the almond tree.

'Please don't go away for ever.'

I stood holding the cage and watching Mr Bull, who began hopping about in the tree. Suddenly he put his head on one side and looked at a flower bud. He nipped it off the twig and mashed it between the two strong snippers of his beak.

'Oh!' I said in horror.

Mr Bull paid no attention but hopped busily about the tree nipping buds off, mashing them up and dropping bits on the ground. He went all over the tree, and before long the bits of bud lay all round me.

'Mr Bull.' I held up his cage. I was thinking of my father. Mr Bull paid no attention to me, not because he could not see me but because he did not want to.

'Mr Bull,' I called very urgently. 'Mr Bull, please.'

Behind me in the house I could hear sounds of people getting up and running baths, yawning and groaning as grown-up people do when they wake up and have to face the world.

Suddenly Mr Bull flipped his wings and flew directly into his cage. Quickly I shut the door and, carrying the cage with Mr Bull in it, I tore back into the house and into my room and shut the door.

'Mr Bull, I don't know what my father will say.'

'I do.'

For the first time since we had met Mr Bull spoke.

'You spoke, Mr Bull.'

'Naturally.'

'Mr Bull, you have ruined my father's almond tree.'

'Nonsense.' Mr Bull hopped down from his perch and drank a sip of water.

'What will he say?'

'He will say I have, or that some other bird has, ruined his almond tree.'

'But you have.'

'Nonsense.'

'Then what do you call what you have done?'

Mr Bull did not answer for a little time, but ate some seed. At last he spoke again, the husks of seed falling out of his beak as the almond buds had done.

'There was a bug in every bud,' he said.

'So you have done good?'

'Naturally.'

'Did you eat the bugs?'

'Yes.'

'How horrid of you.'

'Human beings eat oysters alive, don't they?'

'Yes. Mr Bull, I'm terribly worried about what my father will say.'

'He won't know it's me and next year his tree will flower beautifully.'

'Mr Bull, you have never spoken to me before.'

'It wasn't necessary. Go and have your breakfast.' Mr Bull closed his eyes, tightened his grip on his perch and spoke no more.

My father liked walking round his garden before breakfast to see how his flowers and trees had prospered in the night. He spent as much time as he could in the garden when he was not working at making money in his office in the nearby town. My father said gardening soothed his ulcers.

My mother said to me: 'Hurry up with your breakfast, Kate, or you will be late for school.'

I kept quiet and buried my face in my plate.

My father burst into the room. 'Have you seen the almond tree?' His voice was hoarse.

'No, not yet. Is it lovely' My mother was pouring out a cup of coffee.

'Lovely!' My father's voice rose. 'It's ruined. Some bird has pecked all the buds off it. Blast it!'

'Darling.' My mother made two faces at the same time, which was clever of her, and I decided to practise doing it myself in private. One was the face of loving concern because my father had been upset and was also upsetting his coffee, and the other was the face which meant 'mind the children.'

'It looks as though a blasted bullfinch has been at it. It's ruined. Every bud bitten off and just chucked on the ground.' My father took a great swallow of coffee and choked.

3

'There are no bullfinches in this district.' My mother was trying to be soothing, but she was apt to be right which never soothed my father.

'Goddammit, there must be.'

'Time for school,' my mother said quietly to my sister, and she and I left the room.

'Goddammit, we shall be late,' said my sister outside the room. 'Run.' And she began to run down the road to where we could see the car which gave us a lift each morning waiting for us.

'You are late,' said Andrew from the back seat where he was sitting with his brother James.

'Sorry.' My sister bounded into the car and I followed her. Our neighbour, Mrs Johnson, let in the clutch and drove off.

'Why are you late?' James was rather keen on punctuality. None of the rest of us minded.

'My father's favourite almond tree has had all its buds nipped off by a bullfinch,' said my sister Angela, knowing that just to make such a statement would apprise the Johnson family that our family would be in a state of hypertension and that by tonight my father's ulcers would be giving him hell.

'There are no bullfinches round here.'

Mrs Johnson was a keen bird-watcher, usually heard the first cuckoo, and could tell a warbler's song from a nightingale's. 'Such beautiful birds, I always think. When I was at school in Kent there was a girl who had a canary,' she said.

'Oh, canaries.' Andrew dismissed canaries.

'Didn't you have a pet bullfinch once?' Mrs Johnson called to me across the seat where Angela sat next to her.

'Yes, she had,' Angela answered politely.

I looked at Angela, who is two years older than me, and she did not seem any different from usual, but she had certainly said, 'Yes, she had,' not 'Yes, she has.'

We arrived at our school and Angela went off with Andrew, and James and I went into our part of the school, and all day I wondered whether Mr Bull had really spoken to me and what Angela knew. Lessons passed over my head and I had to depend on James for once, instead of his depending on me, because I am more like my mother than my father: I always know best.

At five we all four climbed into Mrs Johnson's car.

'What's that?' James looked at a book Angela was holding in her lap.

'Oh, just a book on birds.' Angela was rather offhand, as she usually is to people younger than herself.

Mrs Johnson took her eye off the road to look at the book, and we all went tense because we were terrified of accidents.

'Oh,' said Mrs Johnson, 'did you get it from the library? It's that book written by that dreadful man who says bullfinches destroy fruit trees. He must be mad. A whole book written against one small breed of birds. It's nonsense, of course.'

'Is it?' Angela looked sideways at Mrs Johnson.

'Of course it is.'

'Then I won't bother to read it.' Angela threw the book out of the window. Andrew, James and I gasped in admiration.

'Angela! That's a library book.' Mrs Johnson spoke reprovingly. 'We must find it.' She stopped the car and walked back up the road. We followed her, Angela bringing up the rear.

Mrs Johnson picked up the book, which was lying by the side of the road, with some of its pages dog-eared and muddy.

'Angela, you shouldn't do things like that.'

'But you said it was nonsense.'

'It is, but your parents would have to pay the bill for the lost book.'

'Oh, bills.' Angela shoved the book into the glove compartment of Mrs Johnson's car. Her voice sounded just like Andrew's that morning when he had said, 'Oh, canaries.'

When we reached home we both ran upstairs to wash our hands and comb our hair. We always did this if my father's ulcers were going to play him up. Angela came into my room. She looked up at the cage where Mr Bull sat in the evening sunshine, his fat stomach pink and his black head glossy.

'You had better tell me.' Angela stood looking at Mr Bull, who looked back at her sideways with his large brown eye.

'Later.' Mr Bull opened his beak and shut it, snap.

'I suppose this is late enough.' My sister came into my room where I lay in bed. Downstairs we could hear our parents talking.

'He is usually asleep by now,' I said.

'I'm not asleep.'

'Then what's all this about?' I got out of bed and took the cover off Mr Bull's cage.

'Ah.'

'What is it you want?' said Angela. 'Freedom?'

'Preserve me from that.'

'Why?'

'My poor feet.'

'The other birds would attack you,' I said hastily. I did not want to lose Mr Bull.

'Think so?' Mr Bull's chortle was rather offensive.

'He's lazy and greedy. He gets lots of food and care here. Why should he want to go?' said Angela.

'Only sometimes.'

'When?' I asked.

'When the wisteria is in bud, and the apples.'

'A man has written a whole book on how much harm bullfinches do.' Angela and I sat close to the cage. Mr Bull closed his eyes.

'You could go out sometimes early, like this morning,' I said.

'Our father has ulcers,' said Angela.

'Poor fellow.' Mr Bull sounded in no way sympathetic.

'Don't you like him?'

'No.'

'Why not?'

'He doesn't like bullfinches.' Mr Bull sounded very shrewd.

'What good could we do?' Angela suddenly switched her mood to one she occasionally had for doing good works.

'I don't want to do good. I want Mr Bull to have fun,' I said.

Mr Bull was looking at Angela seriously. 'We could warn the others,' he said. 'Hunting and so on.'

'Ah.' I could see Angela mounting a favourite hobby horse. 'Do the others understand you? All the animals and birds who live in fear?'

'Yes. You hunt, don't you?'

'Only because I like riding. Not killing. We shall have to bring the boys in on this. They always know about these things. Their father is a farmer,' said Angela.

'What things?' I choked with jealousy. Mr Bull and Angela seemed to be getting into a partnership which left me out.

'We wouldn't dream of leaving you out.' Mr Bull turned a large, loving eye on me.

'It's sabotage really, isn't it? I adore sabotage.' Angela sat close to the cage. 'The Johnson boys love animals.'

'Take a lot of organizing.' Mr Bull yawned and I felt probably Angela was right and that he was lazy.

'Not if we get help. I know Andrew and James feel as we do. They hate all the unnecessary killing. That's the only reason we like them. But we can't do anything without you.'

'No, you can't, can you?'

'Don't be so complacent just because you live in perfect safety,' snapped Angela.

'What about your cat?'

'With your help we will stop him coming and staring at you. If we can tell the Johnsons' dog not to chase him.'

'I don't like the way he sits and stares,' said Mr Bull. 'He covets me.'

'What are you getting at?' I said to Angela.

'I think she wants a sort of protection racket,' said Mr Bull.

'Protect the persecuted!' I exclaimed, thinking of last week's sermon on television which had so bored me.

'That's about it.' Angela got up and left the room and I heard her talking to our dog who sleeps with her in her room, and calling, 'Vice, Vice, Vice,' in a soft voice. She came back carrying Vice, our cat, in her arms, with Blueprint trotting behind her. Vice fixed Mr Bull with his staring green eyes and Blueprint got up on my bed.

'Stop that, Vice. We know Mr Bull can speak and so can you.'

'What about it?' Vice sounded in no way surprised but began licking his paws and combing his whiskers.

'We want you all to help each other and we will help you.'

'I don't need any help.' Vice went on licking his paws.

'You do when the Johnsons' dog chases you.'

Vice sneezed delicately.

'I'll tell him not to.' Blueprint spoke in a very educated voice considering his antecedents, which were half and half terrier and half and half spaniel.

'I can look after myself,' Vice said prissily.

'A lot of people can't,' said Angela. 'The birds who get nerves when the bird-watchers watch them, the deer, the foxes and the otters who are hunted, the badgers who are dug out of their sets, the birds who are shot.'

'We eat chickens and meat.'

'I know we do, but these things which are done for sport, we could stop those. All the things which upset us.'

'Upset the hunted more,' said Mr Bull coldly.

'I like hunting mice,' said Vice.

'If the Johnsons' dog stopped chasing you, would you stop hunting mice?'

'It is asking rather a lot,' Blueprint said in reasonable tones from my bed.

'It would be terrific fun,' said Vice suddenly. 'Just to upset things.'

'Then will you help?' Angela joined Blueprint on the bed.

'There's a mouse in the wainscot.'

'Then tell him he can come out and you won't hurt him.' Angela spoke cajolingly and Blueprint raised his eyebrows.

'Mouse,' purred Vice. 'Mouse, come on out. I won't hurt you.'

There was a long silence while we waited, and then at last there was a faint scrabble and a very large mouse came out of a very small hole and climbed up Angela's leg on to her lap.

'Ow, you tickled.'

'Sorry.' The mouse looked round at us from Angela's knee and then said: 'I should feel happier in that cage with Mr Bull.'

I opened the door of Mr Bull's cage and the mouse streaked down Angela's leg and up the table leg, across the table and into Mr Bull's cage, where it sat panting, its little sides heaving and its whiskers twitching.

'Don't make a mess,' said Mr Bull to the mouse.

'Do you two know each other?' Angela looked at the mouse looking up at Mr Bull.

'Oh, yes. I eat, well we all eat the seeds Mr Bull scatters about sometimes.'

'Do you all know each other?'

'Only within a certain radius.'

'We shall need the boys to help us organize things,' said Angela to me. 'Their father takes the local paper and knows when and where the hounds are going to meet, and I'm sure he knows about badger baiting and the shooting.'

'Yes,' I said.

Outside we heard the owls hooting.

'They won't help,' said the mouse.

'They might in some ways.' Blueprint was an optimistic dog. 'I'll talk to the Johnsons' dog tomorrow.'

'I thought you always fought,' said Vice.

'It's only noise really, to keep up our status.'

'Status is going to be an obstacle to your game.' Vice finished licking his paws and sat crouched with his eyes shut.

'It will make a start. He told me yesterday that the otter hounds are meeting soon.'

'Where?' exclaimed Angela.

'Find out tomorrow,' said Vice. 'You people can read.'

'Yes. That will mean mounting quite an operation.' I let the mouse out of Mr Bull's cage and he vanished down his hole.

'No manners,' said Vice.

The rest of us said nothing. Angela and Blueprint left the room with Vice, and I covered Mr Bull's cage and snapped out my light because I could hear my parents coming upstairs to bed and my mother saying to my father, 'Do be quiet, you will wake the children.'

'May we have the Johnson boys to tea today? It's Saturday.' Angela sat at the kitchen table eating porridge and watching my mother cooking my father's breakfast.

'I thought you had a war on,' said my father, coming in from the garden.

'That was last week.'

'How fickle you are.' My father picked up the morning paper. 'Just like animals really, excepting dogs of course.' He stroked Blueprint's head. 'Dogs are never fickle. God's finest moral creation.' None of us paid any attention, because if my father had said that dogs were God's finest moral creation once, he had said it a hundred times. Blueprint, however, being of a charitable nature, wagged his tail.

'May we?' said Angela. My mother nodded.

'Now cats,' said my father, 'I admire cats.' He looked at Vice sitting sleekly in the window watching the birds eat the crumbs my mother had thrown out to them. 'Now cats are deep. Did you read last week of some cats killing a child? Remarkable.'

'Dreadful,' said my mother.

'I wonder what the child had done to them,' said Angela.

'I admire cats,' said my father again.

'Not murdering cats, surely, and you a pillar of the law.' My mother neatly slipped two eggs on to a piece of toast and put the plate in front of my father.

'One can have one's days off, I hope,' said my father, a solicitor in the town near which we lived.

'I hope Vice won't kill too many baby birds this year.' My mother looked at Vice who, in spite of his name and cleverness was not a great hunter really.

'There's a spotted flycatcher nesting at the back of the house,' said my father. 'You children are not to go near it. They are shy.'

We nodded agreement.

'Luckily it's quite out of Vice's reach.'

'How is the almond tree?' said Angela, out of pure spite I thought.

'Oh, it will recover. I wouldn't be surprised if it were better than ever next year.' On Saturday mornings, when he doesn't have to go to work, my father is angelic. 'It does trees and plants good to be cut back.'

Vice hopped out of the open window, landing on the path with a flop. The feeding birds did not look up.

'It's almost as if they knew he was not dangerous.' My mother sat down beside my father.

'They would fly off as he sprang and he would look a fool,' muttered Blueprint in a groaning voice.

My father gave Blueprint a piece of bacon.

'Honestly, darling, you shouldn't feed him at meals,' said my mother. Neither my father nor Blueprint paid any attention, and presently, while we reluctantly helped my mother wash up, we saw them going off together for a walk.

'It's absurd,' said my mother. 'He wants to talk to Mr Johnson and he daren't go near their house because the dogs fight.'

'Then he can telephone,' said Angela. 'May I go and ask them to come for the afternoon?' Angela left the kitchen before my mother could answer, leaving me with the washing up.

'She's left me with the washing up,' I said angrily.

'You two are just like animals yourselves.' My mother swished the water down the sink and wrung out the cloth.

'We can read,' I said to myself as I stacked the plates and watched Angela dash past on her bicycle with her behind stuck up in the air.

CALLOWAY COUNTY PUBLIC LIBRARY
710 Main Street
MURRAY, KY 42071

3

After lunch we walked through the wood which separates us from the Johnsons' farm. Blueprint crashed ahead of us, making a lot of noise in the undergrowth, his tail wagging and his whole body shaking from the sheer joy of exercise. Overhead the birds sang rather aggressively and the river rushed in all haste towards the sea.

'Do you think,' I said to Angela, 'that Andrew and James will believe us?'

'They'll have to, won't they?'

'What did you tell them this morning?'

'I just asked them to come for the afternoon and they said they would.'

'You didn't tell them about the animals talking?'

'No.' Angela looked embarrassed.

'Oh,' I said. 'You just asked them to tea?'

'Yes.'

'Oh.'

We walked on, Angela in the lead so that I could not see her face. Ahead of us Blueprint gave a series of excited yelps. We caught up with him to find him dancing rather clumsily round a tree, looking up. Above him, high out of reach, a shadow moved and Angela said crossly: 'Shut up, Blueprint. You mustn't chase squirrels now.'

'Sorry,' said Blueprint. 'I forgot.' He looked sad. 'I shall miss it, it's such fun.'

Blueprint spoke up into the tree. 'We are all going to protect each other and not chase each other any more. Except for fun.'

'Oh yeh?' The squirrel spoke from far above our heads.

'Honestly,' said Blueprint.

'What's up?' Joker, the Johnsons' sheepdog, arrived very silently through the bushes.

'The squirrel won't believe we can all help each other.' Blueprint lifted a leg in token of Joker's arrival, and Joker sniffed and did the same.

'That's because we don't need any help ourselves, or not much. Shall we fight?'

'No, no,' I said.

'Why not? We usually do when you are about.'

'Not now,' said Angela and sat down. 'Are the boys coming?'

'They are ambushing you and getting ready to leap out at you in a moment,' said Joker without turning his head.

'We are too old for that,' said Angela, and I remembered the time when our lives simply were not worth living because the Johnson boys continually ambushed us.

Joker sat down beside Angela, and Blueprint and I joined her.

'Come out, we know you are there.' Angela's voice trembled a little because her heart jumped when people leapt out at her.

The Johnson boys did not answer and Blueprint remarked: 'They know you can't see them. You tell them, Joker.'

Joker trotted off to a deep mass of dead bracken and burrowed in. We heard Andrew laugh and say, 'Oh, Joker, you spoiled it.'

'Come on out,' I called.

Andrew and James crawled out of the bracken and stood brushing bits of it off themselves.

'Why aren't the dogs fighting?' James spoke in tones of amazement.

'Come and sit down and we'll tell you why.'

The boys came and sat near us with Joker. Blueprint sat beside us, panting a little, his eyes half shut in the sunshine. There was a long pause and nobody spoke. The river cast itself against the stones and rocks, poured into pools, swung round corners, threw up little bits of spray, and all round us in the wood the birds sang heartily. I looked at Angela and she looked at me. The two dogs seemed to be grinning slightly.

A piece of stick fell on Andrew's head.

'Who threw that?'

'I did.' A tiny voice spoke from above our heads. Blueprint stood up and put his paws up a tree-trunk.

'If I'm not to chase you, you must not tease us.' He looked up the tree-trunk and spoke in a very reasonable voice.

Andrew looked at James and at us and then looked quickly away. Joker licked his face. 'It's all right. We all know.'

'All know what?'

'Well, Kate's bullfinch, having nothing better to do, has let on that we can speak.'

'How terribly awkward,' James exclaimed.

'Why?' said Angela.

'Well, our poor parents.'

'Our parents don't know, only us.'

'I mean, just think of the things my father says in front of the cows and the sheep, and as for the pigs – ' Words failed James.

'That's why we asked you to tea to discuss things,' said Angela. 'Awkward it certainly is in some ways, but most helpful in others.'

'Only you four know.' Blueprint rolled lazily on his back and made a sudden effort to catch his tail.

'It's a terrible responsibility.' Andrew looked at Angela.

'Rot,' said Angela. 'Just think of the fun we can have, preventing things.'

'Preventing what?' James could be very obtuse.

'Otter hunting, fox hunting, deer hunting, shooting, all sorts of things.'

'Shall we be able to stop the foxes eating my father's lambs?'

'We can try.'

'Badger baiting,' I said. I knew Andrew was terribly fond of badgers.

'That would be something.'

'And otters.'

'There are no otters here, alas.'

'Oh, yes there are. There's an otter with his wife and children only ten yards from where you are sitting.' The squirrel had come down the bole of the tree and hung downwards, poised.

'How marvellous!' Andrew exclaimed.

'Not if the hounds come this way,' I said. 'It won't be marvellous then.'

'We must save them,' Andrew said firmly.

'When are the hounds meeting?'

'Soon, I think. I heard my father say so. He said something about it only yesterday. He said they come over his land and make a lot of noise and they are killing off all the otters in the rivers.'

'Does he mind?'

'Not enough to do anything about it. He doesn't fish and he's very busy.'

'About time we got busy.' Andrew turned to James. 'Dash home and look at the paper and we'll wait for you here.'

'They bring the hounds in a van,' James said gloomily. 'And they all dress up in that archaic uniform and carry long sticks. The otters don't stand a chance.'

'Do go, James,' I said.

James hesitated and then ran off through the wood back towards the farm.

'How are we going to get in touch with the otters?' I asked.

'Ask Vice and Mr Bull,' Angela said crossly. 'They will know what to do. They hunt a whole long stretch of the river, miles of it in one day. There may be other otters besides these.'

'It isn't going to be easy,' I said.

'But it's going to be fun.' Andrew stroked Joker's head and Joker gazed into his eyes, saying nothing.

Presently we heard James coming back and the dogs wagged their tails and pricked their ears.

'Next Saturday at Overton.' James was panting slightly.

'Overton.' Andrew got up. 'Come on, we must see Mr Bull. Joker, you go home. We must keep up appearances.'

'Oh Lord, do you mean Blueprint and I have to pretend to fight every time we meet?'

'Only if grown-up people are there.'

'What a bore.'

'And Joker, please don't chase Vice any more,' I said.

'Not chase Vice!' Joker sounded shocked. 'I take care never to catch him. To be honest, I wouldn't know what to do if I did.'

'No cat chasing,' said Andrew.

'That means no fun.'

'Oh, we'll see we all get our fun.'

Joker looked doubtful, but then left us, and the two boys and Blueprint came back to our house with us. We all went up to my room where Mr Bull was sitting in the sun in his cage and Vice was lying asleep in a close ball on my bed.

'Mr Bull,' I said.

'Must you all come tramping in? This is when I have my nap'

'Mr Bull, we want your advice.'

'Oh, do you?'

'Please, Mr Bull.'

'You forgot my groundsel today.' On the bed Vice yawned.

'Mr Bull, we find there is a family of otters by the river in the wood.'

'What about it?'

'The otter hounds are meeting at Overton next Saturday. They will hunt the river from there right past here.'

'I daresay they will.' Mr Bull spoke carelessly. 'Doesn't worry me,' he added.

'It worries us.' Andrew sat near the cage. 'How can we stop them?'

'You can't.'

'But they will kill the otters.'

'Not if they aren't there.'

'What do you mean?'

16

'I mean the otters must be hidden where the hounds can't find them. It's quite simple.'

'Is it?' Andrew looked anxious. 'Who is going to tell the otters?'

'I had better,' said Vice lazily. 'I'll tell them tonight on my prowl.'

'Our mother is trying to stop you prowling because of the young birds,' I said.

'Oh that,' Vice said rudely. 'I'll tell them and we must send word upstream and downstream too to other otters.'

'Who can do that?'

'The owls. They fly up the valley and down.'

'Can't we meet the otters?' Andrew asked patiently.

'It may come to that. I must think it out. Run along now and I'll give you all your instructions tomorrow.' Mr Bull closed his eyes, lifted one foot up among his stomach feathers and crouched down broodily. We left the room and went out and into the wood again.

'Old codger,' said James.

'We can't do without him,' I said.

'Did you see Vice just go to sleep again as we left?' Andrew was laughing.

Angela was watching a trout cruising slowly in the river. 'I think we had better leave it to Mr Bull and Vice to think out. We can try and think of a safe hiding place, if they will trust us.'

'Blueprint,' Andrew stroked Blueprint's head. 'Do you know where the otters are?'

'Oh yes,' Blueprint answered politely.

'Can't you show us?'

'No. They are afraid of me and of you.'

'Extra hemp,' I exclaimed suddenly.

'Yes,' said Angela. 'Bribery is the only thing.'

'Only a week is a very short time.' James's voice was reedy with anxiety.

We all sat on the bank brooding, worried to death for the otters we had never seen.

'Could we get at the hounds?'

'No, Andrew. They live too far away.'

'Tea-time,' said Angela.

We all got up and wandered towards our house.

'Tea is ready,' our mother called unnecessarily when she saw us. We all ate tea, politely passing plates to each other and thanking each other effusively. My mother looked at us suspiciously from time to time and I knew she thought we had quarrelled.

'Hullo,' my father said as he came into the room. 'Just going to cast a line. Coming, Blueprint?' Blueprint followed my father out of the room.

'Fish?' queried Andrew.

Angela nodded. We finished our tea and went out and leant on the bridge and watched our father walking down the river with his rod. Blueprint ran ahead of him and we could hear his barking voice shouting: 'Don't rise, don't rise.'

'*He* doesn't like eating them, *I* do.' Vice slipped past us into the wood.

Presently we heard my father cursing Blueprint and sounds of splashing.

'I think he's overdoing it,' I said.

'No, he isn't. It's good psychology. If the otters see the fish have been warned they will listen to Vice.' Andrew listened to my father 'Fine turn of phrase,' he added.

'It cuts both ways. The otters like fish too.' James spoke a little sadly.

'Let's all meet in the wood tonight,' said Angela. 'We can bring Mr Bull in his cage, then he will feel safe and wise, and you bring Joker. No doubt the cats will meet us at midnight.' Angela likes a bit of drama. We could just as easily have met at midday the following day.

We did meet at midnight in the middle of the wood. We had torches and so did Andrew and James. I carried Mr Bull's cage with a cover over it. Blueprint and Joker came with us and the boys respectively; Vice appeared out of the dark, and the Johnsons' tom cat. We sat down and I put Mr Bull's cage in the middle of our group.

'It's cold,' said Joker. 'Hurry up.'

'I've told the otters,' said Vice. 'They are going to think it over.'

'Think it over! Good Lord, they surely trust us?'

'No.'

'I told you they wouldn't.'

'They will.' Mr Bull spoke from under the cover of his cage and sneezed. 'It is cold,' he added. 'I shall get a chill.'

'What next?' Andrew pulled his sweater up round his ears.

'Keep still and listen.' Mr Bull let out several pipes and chortles and a low 'Whoo' came from above our heads.

'We won't eat you,' said Vice.

'What about my mice?' The owl sounded rather difficult. 'What do I get if I warn the otters?'

'I'll buy you something nice with my pocket money,' said Andrew.

'All right. I'll tell the owls to carry the news up and down the valley.'

'They need more than news. They must all be told to come here to be hidden.'

'They won't like it.' Vice sounded bored.

'That or the hounds,' said Mr Bull.

'That or the hounds.' A voice we had not heard before spoke from outside our circle. Blueprint and Joker craned their necks.

'No chasing,' said Mr Bull as though he could see the dogs. The otter sniggered.

'Cut-throats.' His voice scarcely reached us.

'The children are not cut-throats.' Blueprint was fair and reasonable. 'And didn't you see me warning the trout this evening?'

'Oh, I did. You looked a proper Charlie, and I had to go miles to get the wife and children's supper.'

'Anyway' – Angela ignored the unseen otter – 'will you spread the news?' She looked up to where she thought the owl sat.

'Okay.' We heard the owl leave its branch, and then there was silence.

'Every bird, every animal must be told. Now take me home. I'm cold.'

I carried Mr Bull back to the house and tried to speak to him as I went.

'Shut up,' he said snappily.

'Why?'

'I'm speaking to the bats.'

Angela and I slipped into the house with Vice and Blueprint at our heels.

'Will it work?'

'We can but try.' Angela sounded depressed.

In the morning I put Mr Bull's cage by the open window and got back into bed. Mr Bull started piping and chortling and before long the garden birds were flying past the window or sometimes stopping on the window-sill to listen. I watched bemused as chaffinch, sparrow, thrush, blackbird and tits visited in quick succession, and then with a flutter of wings a swallow followed by a martin.

'That takes care of the birds.' Mr Bull sounded pleased with himself.

'What will they do?'

'Each bird will tell its opposite number at the edge of its territory, and the news will spread like a ripple.'

'What about the animals?'

'Vice is going to tell foxes, rabbits, badgers and all farm animals.'

'Will they let us help them, Mr Bull?'

'Oh, I think so.'

'Would you like some extra hemp?'

'You know it upsets me.'

'What can I do then to thank you?'

'Let me out.'

'I can't for long. They will be getting up.'

'Just for a short time.'

I opened the cage and watched Mr Bull flip over the window ledge on to the wisteria which grew along the house. Snip, snip, snip went his beak.

'You'll give us away,' I hissed.

'Pick up the bits then.'

I tore down through the still sleeping house and ran round to below my window and as the bits of bud fell I furtively gathered them up.

'Victim of a small bird.' Vice passed me on the path and vanished among the bushes.

Presently I saw Mr Bull flit back through my window into his cage. Angela looked at me from my room, laughed and shut the window. I ran to the stream and threw the buds into it and then raced back to the house and dressed for breakfast.

'I hear the otter hounds are meeting at Overton next weekend,' said my father with his mouth full.

'Mr Johnson won't be pleased. His sheep haven't finished lambing.' My mother looked up from a letter she was reading.

'Silly waste of time and money,' said my father. 'There isn't an otter within miles.'

'One never knows. They are very secretive,' said my mother. Then she added: 'Have any fun last night fishing?'

'Not a rise. There are plenty of fish about though. I saw them. I shan't take Blueprint with me again. He acted like a lunatic, rushing in and out of the water barking.'

'Poor boy, he's not very bright.' My mother stroked Blueprint's head and Angela and I exchanged looks.

'Can't we ask these otter people not to go through our land?' asked Angela.

'Not really. There aren't any otters and they do no harm. Besides' – my father buttered a piece of toast – 'that fellow who is the M.O.H. does a lot of business through us. I don't want to offend him.'

'Easily offended?' enquired my mother.

'Oh, stuffy. He's quarrelled with every firm in the country except ours. I don't want to lose him. We have the girls to educate after all.'

'I love otters,' said my mother vaguely.

'I hate them being hunted,' said Angela snappily.

'Oh, live and let live.' My father smiled.

'Turn a blind eye do you mean?'

'Exactly.'

'What would you do if you saw an otter being torn to bits?' Angela was becoming aggressive.

'Be a bit late to do anything then, wouldn't it?' My father spoke casually.

'They are a lot of murderers,' I said.

'No, darling, they are not. Most hunting people are passionately devoted to animals. The R.S.P.C.A. depend on them, you know.'

'If I saw an otter being hunted and it took refuge in my house, say, I wouldn't open the door to the hounds,' said my father, helping himself to marmalade with his knife, which is a thing he knew my mother hated because she put a perfectly good spoon by the pot.

'Hardly a likely supposition,' said my mother, pushing the spoon too late towards my father.

'May we go now?' Angela got up.

'Yes,' said my mother unexpectedly, because usually she made us help wash up.

'We must get them into the house and hide them until it's safe for them to go back,' said Angela to me as we went upstairs.

'What about the smell?' I said.

'What smell?'

'The otter smell, stupid. The hounds will follow them to the house.' We went to my room.

'What can we do about the smell, Mr Bull, if we shelter the otters next Saturday in the house?'

'Carry them into the house.'

'Then we shall smell.'

'Wash in carbolic.'

'What a noise the birds are making.' Angela leant out of the window. 'Listen.'

I joined her and listened. All the birds were singing their hearts out and the swallows swooped in great arcs across the sky. High above us a pair of buzzards wheeled and screamed.

'Are they passing messages?' Angela looked at Mr Bull.

'Yes.'

We listened for quite a long time.

'They will need reminding all the time. They forget so easily.' Angela was looking at the ravaged wisteria.

'Look, here comes James.'

James waved from where he stood at the edge of the wood. He wore gumboots, jeans and a thick jersey.

'What's up?' Angela enquired.

'Come into the wood.'

We followed James.

'James, you've got something odd under your jersey.'

'I'm not odd,' said an animal voice.

'Well, you show.'

The bulge under James's jersey shifted shape and said: 'That better?'

'No, you still show.'

'Have you got a kitten in there?' I asked.

'No, an otter.'

We gasped with respect and awe and watched the bulge under James's jersey change shape until James seemed to have one huge lump, then elongate itself until he looked as though he had a French loaf under his jersey, then wriggle again and a whiskered face peered out at his waist line.

'Isn't he gorgeous?' said James.

'Marvellous,' we whispered, watching the otter scramble down James's leg on to the ground.

'I went to the otters and asked if they would conceal themselves about our persons,' said James.

'It won't do,' said Angela. 'Mr Bull says they must come into the house and we must overlay their scent with carbolic or something smelly.'

'The house!' The otter sounded horrified. 'I've a perfectly good house of my own.'

'The hounds will get you there,' I said.

'What does your wife say?' said Angela quickly.

'Oh, she's worried to death. The children are so small.'

'All into the house,' said James firmly. The otter looked disgusted.

'We are only trying to help,' I said.

'But the house, it's a terrible idea.'

'Not so bad as death,' said Angela.

'Almost.' The otter did not sound in any way grateful.

I looked at the otter. 'Are there other otters up and down the river?' I asked.

'Yes, but we don't speak.'

'Then they will be in danger too.'

'I suppose so.'

'We must save them.'

'Why, if you save us?'

'No otters should be killed.'

'Both lots upstream and down have better fishing and hunting than we do.'

'How can you be so selfish!' exclaimed Angela. The otter turned round and disappeared into the wood.

'Now you've offended him,' said James.

'What are we to do?' I ground my teeth.

'Ask the dogs to go up river and down and tell all the otters to come here. Then we will hide them while the hunt is on.'

'Blueprint!' Angela called at the top of her voice.

'Yes.' Blueprint appeared, as he always did, looking cheerful and eager.

'Blueprint, will you and Joker go and tell the otters upstream and down to come to us on Friday night and we will shelter them while the hunt is on?'

Blueprint did not answer but thundered away through the wood towards the Johnsons' farm.

'Our father does business for the Master of the Otter Hounds,' said Angela gloomily.

'Well, my father is in the middle of selling him a cow.'

'Our father said if he had a house full of otters he would turn a blind eye,' Angela said loyally.

'Well, he's a lawyer,' said James, and I wondered what the Johnsons said about our family in the privacy of their house.

All that week we were rather distracted. Only Mr Bull seemed perfectly calm when we came home in the evenings.

Andrew spent some of his pocket money buying steak which he put in the wood for the owls. My mother complained that Vice was prowling at night and had an argument with my father who said it couldn't be helped and it was 'cat nature'.

'Don't look so fussed. They have all been warned,' said Mr Bull.

'Which room shall we put them in when they come?' I asked.

'If they come.'

'Surely they will?'

Angela went to the village on her bicycle and bought some Jeyes fluid.

'Mother will be furious,' I said.

'I will roll in something she thinks really foul,' said Blueprint, 'and then you can wash me in the Jeyes.'

'Oh, Blueprint, you are heroic,' I said, because Blueprint couldn't stand baths.

'I'll get Joker to do the same.' Blueprint swelled with pride at being called heroic.

'I shall get the tom cat from the farm to help me,' said Vice mysteriously.

'What does he mean?' Angela's anxiety was dulling her intelligence.

'Nothing like a tom cat for sheer stink,' said Mr Bull.

'Our poor mother,' I said. 'And my room,' I insisted. 'Then they will have Mr Bull and they can feel they can climb down the wisteria if they must.'

'All this is pure hypothesis,' said Mr Bull.

'What do you mean?'

'They are unlikely to come.'

'Why? We've warned them enough.'

'Oh, warnings.' Mr Bull went to sleep.

'The hounds are meeting at ten-thirty. They should get here about twelve.' Andrew pointed with his finger at the winding river on the ordnance map. 'One or two of us should go to the meet, one of us should stay here and one walk up river with the dogs.'

'But all the otters will be here.'

'Mr Bull doesn't think so. I agree with him. If they come at all it will be at the last possible minute.'

'Don't be so pessimistic, Andrew.'

'I'm realistic.'

'Vice,' I said, 'what do the otters think?'

'They have all been warned, but whether they will act is another thing.'

We cast lots and it fell to James and Andrew to go to the meet, to Angela to walk up river and for me to wait near the house to admit the otters.

'They should all come the night before,' I said.

'They won't,' said the mouse who had joined us. 'They are not house-minded, not civilized.'

'We can only hope for the best.'

Blueprint laid his heavy head on my knee and groaned.

On the morning of the Saturday we saw Andrew and James go by, walking up the river with Joker. Angela followed them with Blueprint, and I went down to the river in the wood.

It was a beautiful morning. I just sat and waited, feeling tears of disappointment very close. No otters had come the night before, it was already eleven and the hounds would be moving downstream, nosing in and out of the banks, egged on by all those people carrying long sticks to block the way of any otter trying to escape with its life through the shallows. I looked at my watch. Eleven-thirty. Vice joined me, sitting with his ears pricked and paws neatly together.

'Here they come,' he said.

'I can hear nothing.'

'I can.'

'Then beg the otters to come.'

Vice went off with his tail in the air and I sat rigid.

Presently in the water I saw a ripple and an otter's head peered at me from behind a stone.

'This the sanctuary?'

'Yes. Do hurry.'

A pair of otters slipped out of the river on to the grass and followed me through the wood. I led them to the back of the house and upstairs to my bedroom.

'Get into the cupboard,' said Mr Bull. 'That's right. Be sensible.'

The otters climbed furtively into my cupboard and I shut the door.

'Where are the babies, Mr Bull?'

'Oh, that's not our lot. Those come from miles downstream. Our lot have three babies who are too small to leave.'

'Why didn't they say so?'

'Can't expect everything,' said Mr Bull.

'I'll fetch them,' I said. Far up the river I could hear the sound of the hounds baying.

'Our lot think themselves clever. It's a great drawback.' Mr Bull pecked at his seed and drank a sip of water.

'Mr Bull, how can you?'

'It's not me they are hunting.'

'Vice has gone to tell them,' I said.

'They don't care for Vice.' Mr Bull, safe in his cage, was complacent. I left him and hurried back to the wood where I met Vice sauntering towards me with his tail in the air.

'Vice, where are they?'

'All in their hole.' Vice yawned and rolled on his back, stretching out a paw towards me.

'Vice, please show me where they are.'

Vice got up and led the way through the trees to the edge of the river. 'Here,' he said.

I saw a hole I had passed a hundred times.

'In there?' I was incredulous.

'Yep.'

'Otters!' I called.

There was a long silence and then an otter's voice said: 'What do you want?'

'I want to hide you and your wife and family. The hounds are coming. Can't you hear them?'

'Oh yes, we hear them.'

'Do come.'

'Where?'

'I already have two otters safe in my room with Mr Bull. Do come.'

'I'll ask the wife.'

I waited. The water carried the sound of the hounds downstream, and I seemed to hear Blueprint's voice and Joker's too. I wondered whether they could have become over-excited and joined in the hunt.

'Here we are.'

Two otters, each carrying a very small baby, emerged from the hole.

'Hurry,' I said.

'One more,' said one of the otters, and vanished down the hole again, reappearing quickly with the third baby.

'You'll have to let me carry it.' I snatched the baby from the ground and hurried up the river towards our house. Behind me Vice's venomous voice said: 'Hurry, you fools.'

On the bridge by our house our mother and father were standing looking upstream. I heard my father say: 'It disturbs the fish.'

'I should think it would disturb the otters more,' my mother said acidly.

'Oh, there aren't any otters on this stretch of river. I asked Johnson and he ought to know.'

I ran across the lane and into our house and up the stairs to my room. I reached it at the same time as the otters. Vice brought up the rear.

'Put them in the chest of drawers,' said Mr Bull.

'Why not with the others?' I said.

'They aren't on speaking terms.'

I opened the bottom drawer and the female otter leapt in with the baby in her mouth, followed by her mate. I shoved the third baby in after them and shut the drawer. Vice was already leaving the room. I saw him dashing downstairs. As I went out of the side door I had come in by I smelt a fearful smell.

'Was that you, Vice?'

'Yes. The Johnsons' cat has done the front door.'

'My poor mother!'

'Who do you want to please?' Vice ran off into the wood.

I joined my parents on the bridge, my heart thumping. Upstream, coming down quickly, we could hear hounds, and Blueprint and Joker barking.

'Sounds like Blueprint,' said my mother.

'He went out with Angela,' I said.

'He'll try and fight the hounds,' said my father. 'They will massacre him.' My father had pride in Blueprint's fighting capacities.

'Oh, the poor otters!' I said.

'But there aren't any, darling. It's just a lot of show.'

I thought of all the otters in my bedroom, and the family Mr Bull said lived upstream. They certainly would be dead.

Angela came walking down the river bank her eyes shining. She hurried into the house and I went after her. 'Ooh, what a pong! Where are the otters?'

'One lot in my cupboard and one in the chest of drawers,' I said.

'Okay.' Angela fished under her jersey and brought out two tiny otters and put them into the middle drawer.

'You babies keep quiet,' said Mr Bull.

We shut the drawer and ran down the stairs. 'Where are the parents? Are they dead?' I asked.

'No. Andrew's got them in his gumboots. Hurry.'

We reached the bridge in time to see the pack of hounds milling round and under it and among them Joker and Blueprint barking their heads off. Above the clamour I heard Blueprint shout into a large hound's ear: 'Louder, louder, and carry on downstream.' The hound, who appeared rather a jolly sort of animal, gave a tremendous bay, throwing up his head as he did so. All the other hounds joined in joyously.

'I wonder what they think they are hunting,' shouted my father to my mother.

'Otters,' shouted my mother to my father.

'Rubbish,' shouted my father. 'I told you Johnson says there are no otters on this stretch of river.'

'So you did, darling,' my mother mouthed. 'Here come the Johnson boys. Oh, poor Andrew, what's happened?'

Andrew, his feet bare and jeans wet, limped along the bank. 'Tally ho! and all that lark,' he said. He was carrying his gumboots. 'I filled my gumboots.'

'Go into the house and borrow mine,' said my mother.

Andrew went barefoot up the short bit of lane and into our house. 'What a stink! Where are the babies, Angela?'

'In my chest of drawers,' I said.

'What a stink,' he repeated, handing his gumboots to Angela, who hurried upstairs with them.

'It's the cats' contribution,' I said, watching Andrew put on my mother's boots. 'What happened?'

'We got them just before the hounds. Angela grabbed the two babies and I put the grown ones in my boots.'

'Where are the human hunters?' I asked.

'Coming along nicely,' said Andrew.

We went out and rejoined our parents by the bridge. Some three dozen people, some dressed in hunting uniforms carrying long sticks, were moving about. My parents were pointing downstream towards the distant sound of hounds baying.

Blueprint came trotting home panting, his eyes shining and his tongue lolling.

'Blueprint has rolled in something terrible,' said Angela.

'Oh Lord, we must bath him and he does so hate it.'

'The whole house smells,' remarked my father. 'Very curious. I'm going out.'

'He's afraid of being asked to bath Blueprint,' said my mother. 'Give me a hand, Angela, and Kate, will you open the windows, the smell is rather much.'

Angela and my mother took Blueprint into the scullery. Andrew, James and I dashed upstairs to my room.

'Better let them all go now while your father is out and your mother busy,' remarked Mr Bull.

We opened my cupboard and the drawers and the otters streamed out and down the stairs. I carried the extra baby in my hand as far as the otters' hole, put it down and turned away. None of the otters had said 'thank you'; they had just slipped away into the river.

Far away downstream the big hound was baying.

'Those hounds think this the funniest thing that's ever happened,' remarked Joker in a superior tone, and he trotted away towards the farm.

My mother went out during the afternoon to see Mrs Johnson. Angela and I walked down through the wood towards the Johnson farm.

'An ungrateful lot,' said Angela.

'They had their mouths full of babies,' I said.

'Even so.'

'Even so I would help them again.'

'What we need is a car,' said Angela.

'Why?'

'Well, I don't altogether rely on the birds and animals. A car to get about in is what we need.'

We met the Johnson boys sitting by the river, both silent.

'You look glum,' I said.

'We missed so much.'

'What do you mean?'

'We missed my father having a tearing row with the hunting people for disturbing the sheep.'

'The sheep knew. Joker told them.'

'They acted disturbed and my father was worried to death. What he said to the man who fell in the river would blister the paint off a battleship.'

'How lovely,' we said.

'Why did the man fall in the river?'

'Joker tripped him for fun.'

'Good for Joker.'

'What we need is a car,' said Andrew.

'Just what I was saying,' said Angela. 'The animals are too frivolous.'

'It isn't that. The real trouble is that they all seem to hunt each other and simply do not worry about others, only themselves.'

We all became very thoughtful.

'None of us is large enough to drive,' said James.

'I shall go and speak to Tom Foley,' said Andrew.

'Andrew!' we all exclaimed with one voice.

'Well, why not?'

Why not indeed. We all looked at each other in horror.

'Father says he's an intellectual.'

'He can drive, he has a car, he's – well he's the sort of person who would help. What's an intellectual?'

We all sat and thought about Tom Foley. Tom Foley so often fined for poaching salmon. Tom Foley up before the magistrates for driving an unlicensed car. Tom Foley and sheep – he had a funny way with sheep. Had we not all been brought up to keep out of Tom Foley's way?

'He has a dog,' said James.

'He has carrier pigeons,' said Andrew.

'He's got a girl friend,' said Angela.

'Never!' I exclaimed.

'He has,' said Angela.

'Who is it?' said Andrew.

'Nobody we know.'

'I think I'll go and see him just the same,' said Andrew.

'We are not allowed to talk to him,' said Angela.

'That wouldn't matter. Didn't you notice today that only the dogs were reliable? Tom's dog would be reliable.'

'She couldn't drive a car,' said James. 'When Tom's drunk,' he added. 'Or being intellectual. I don't think it's a disease.'

'Or even if he were not,' I said.

'The village is too public,' said Angela.

'Then I must see him at home.'

'Don't be stupid. None of us knows where he lives.'

'He always says "roundabout" when anyone asks him.'

'Some animal or bird would know.'

'Would they tell us?'

'Good heavens, now that we saved their lives!'

'That isn't what they think.'

'They don't think we saved their lives?'

'No. Blueprint says the last thing he heard from the otters was one otter saying to the other that our behaviour was unwarrantable interference.'

'I thought so,' said James sadly. 'They all think we are cranks.'

'All the more reason to get Tom Foley to help. He's a crank if ever there was one.' Angela got up from the long grass she was sitting in and felt her damp behind. 'It's damp,' she said.

'Who said Tom had a girl friend?' I asked.

'My father,' said James. 'Long ago, some time last summer, I heard my father telling my mother that Tom Foley had been thrown out of the pub because he was tipsy.'

'What's that got to do with a girl friend?'

'I don't know, only my father laughed and said Tom cursed them all in the pub and said he was off with his girl friend.'

'He doesn't seem to me the type to have a girl friend.' Andrew stood up too.

'That's what my father said.'

'Have any of us seen her?' I asked, looking round.

'No,' the others all answered at once.

'What do we know about him?' James could be quite good at sticking to the point.

'We know he lives somewhere near here,' said Angela.

'We know he hates the law.' I spoke as a lawyer's daughter. 'Our father says he's a law unto himself.'

'We know he's marvellous with sheep,' Andrew continued. 'He always doctors ours and he always helps with the shearing and he's a dab hand with delicate lambs.'

'Yes,' I said.

'We know he has a car, a vintage car.' James spoke respectfully.

'I believe he only works to get the money for its petrol and oil,' said Andrew. 'These boots are your mother's. I must return them. Lucky she has large feet.'

'It's a Bull-nosed Morris,' said James, who adores cars.

'He could make a lot of money if he sold it,' I said.

'But we want to use it.'

'Well, then, first we must find him. Would Mr Bull know?' Andrew queried.

'I'll ask him,' I said. 'If he doesn't he could find out.'

'I'm puzzled about his girl friend.' Andrew didn't trust many people.

'She's called Floss,' said Joker, who had joined the boys as we talked.

'Floss what? An odd name for a girl.'

'Floss,' repeated Joker, looking intelligently down his long nose. Joker is one of those black and white collies who go creepy-crawly round the sheep and bemuse them into going into pens.

'Floss,' he said again and yawned.

'I'll go and ask Mr Bull now,' I said, and I left the others and went home and up to my room.

Mr Bull was sitting in his cage with the afternoon sun shining on him, so that I could see and admire his glossy black head and deep pink stomach.

'You look beautiful, Mr Bull.'

'I am.'

'Mr Bull, do you know where Tom Foley lives?'

'He gets drunk. He's peculiar. He writes, so they say.'

'We know that's what they say, but he might help, Mr Bull. He has a car.'

'Very old.'

'I know it's old but it works. Do you think he would help us?'

'You could ask him.'

'Where does he live?'

'Everyone knows.'

'We don't.'

'You have been told to keep away from him. I heard your mother – '

'That's because of his language, Mr Bull. The boys know him.'

'But not where he lives.'

'No.'

Mr Bull opened his beak and let out a series of chortles and pipes, then stopped and seemed to go to sleep.

'Do tell me, Mr Bull.' I felt that if Mr Bull went on being so complacent I would do something nasty to him.

'No, you wouldn't.' He opened his eyes.

'Wouldn't what?'

'Do anything nasty.'

I began to laugh and said: 'You are too clever, Mr Bull. Too clever by half.'

'By half what?'

'Tell me, Mr Bull – please.'

'Tom Foley lives in the big wood on the hill above the Johnsons' farm.'

'But that's National Trust. A nature reserve.'

'Doesn't make any difference.'

'It's huge. How can we find him?'

'Get Joker or Blueprint to lead you there. They know.'

'What devils not to tell us,' I said.

'Perhaps you didn't ask them.'

I found Angela and the two Johnson boys standing where I had left them. Joker was sitting beside them and Blueprint with his ears pricked and head on one side. As I reached them Vice came sauntering down the path licking his lips.

'Vice! What have you eaten?' Angela asked suddenly.

'It fell out of the nest,' Vice answered casually. 'Only a young thrush, nothing rare. They are at their best before they can fly.'

'I don't call that helping each other.' Angela was furious.

'I was helping myself.' Vice sounded in no way perturbed. 'And the thrushes, of course. It had hurt its wing falling, poor thing. It makes one mouth less to feed for the parents.'

Vice sat down beside Joker and closed his eyes, his long white whiskers spreading out from beside his nose like the strings of a lyre.

Andrew shrugged his shoulders and said: 'Did Mr Bull tell you where Tom Foley lives?'

'He said everyone knows,' I said rather spitefully. 'Everyone except us, of course. He said Joker would lead us there. He lives in the High Woods above the Johnsons.'

'Joker.' James looked at Joker, who wagged his tail, rolled his eyes and looked amused and contrite all at once.

'We none of us asked him,' I said.

'Nor did we.' Andrew stroked Joker, who was standing up against him now with his paws on his chest, trying to reach his face to lick.

'You didn't ask me either.' Blueprint pressed his rather barrel-shaped body against my legs.

'And Vice knows too, I suppose,' said Angela.

'Naturally.' Vice purred more to himself than to us as he sat in the sun with his tail wrapped round him, absolutely still except for the tip of his tail which went flip, flip gently.

'Andrew looked at his watch. 'If we went now?'

'Yes, at once,' said Angela. 'You dogs lead us, and you,' she turned suddenly on Vice, 'you go home.' She bent to look into Vice's face. Like lightning he shot out a paw and scratched her cheek, then with his tail in the air he ambled off towards home.

'Never mind,' Blueprint said to her. 'We will lead you to Tom Foley.'

We followed the dogs past the Johnsons' farmhouse and waved to our mothers who were sitting on the doorstep in the sun.

'Going for a walk?' my mother called.

'Yes, sort of,' we waved back. My mother is a town person and has never realized that country people do not ever go for a walk. They walk for a sound purpose. Joker and Blueprint, their tails high, led us through the Johnsons' pasture, past the sheep who scarcely stopped munching grass to look at us, and up into the High Woods.

A cart-track led for a quarter of a mile to an old quarry. Ahead of us up the hill the wood stretched, oaks and beeches, larch and hazel, with a thick undergrowth of bramble and bracken. We had often played in the quarry and knew it well, but the wood was so thick and the brambles so thorny that we had not often gone far into it.

Joker led the way up the hill, in and out of the undergrowth, the white tip of his tail held high. Blueprint followed, sniffing the air. We followed in Indian file, only hearing the sound of the dry twigs crackling under our feet and the birds high above us in the trees. Somewhere a cuckoo cuckooed boringly and incessantly and a woodpecker startled us with a loud shriek of laughter.

Suddenly we were standing on the edge of a clearing, the four of us in a row, and the dogs standing by us wagging their tails and panting slightly.

'It's a badgers' set,' said Andrew under his breath.

All round us were well-established badgers' sets. In the middle of the clearing was a patch of grass, and lying on his back, with a very old brown hat over his eyes, a man asleep. His left hand and arm lovingly encircled a small dog who was watching us with very bright intelligent eyes peering down a sharp pointed nose. Her ears were pricked and her expression enigmatic. Above us the woodpecker let out another shriek of lunatic laughter and a pair of jays began to tease. The man stirred, automatically stroking the dog's silky flank.

Joker trotted down towards the man and appeared to be saying something friendly to the little bitch. She bared her teeth in a silent snarl and laid back her ears. Joker retreated a couple of yards and sat down.

'It's Tom Foley,' said James.

The man sat up, rubbed his eyes and looked up at us.

'Well?' said Tom Foley.

Joker wagged his tail.

'May we come and talk to you?' Andrew stepped forward.

'Free country.' Tom Foley stroked his dog. 'In parts,' he added. 'Not many parts left.'

'It's that sort of thing we wanted to talk to you about.'

'Yes?' Tom Foley was not exactly forthcoming.

'We need help.' Angela walked down into the hollow and sat beside Joker.

'Ask your father, he's a lawyer.'

'It's not a legal matter. No need to be huffy.'

Tom went on stroking his dog, who went on looking at us with her very bright eyes.

We all drew close to Tom who was now sitting up and looking at us with amusement down a long wandering nose, out of small eyes, which curiously resembled his dog's. We all stared and sat silent. I appraised Tom Foley's clothes. The hat I recognized at once as Mr Johnson's. He called it his Milk Marketing Board hat, and there had been considerable uproar on the last occasion he had wished to wear it and no one had been able to find it. The suit puzzled me as I knew I had seen it before.

'Parson's country gentleman Honest to God Christian outfit,' muttered Blueprint in my ear, and went on, 'shoes from Lobb's, shirt Marks and Sparks, tie from the jumble sale.'

'Who is Lobb?' I whispered.

'Everyone knows that,' grunted Blueprint in an unconvincing voice.

'Know me again, won't you.' Tom Foley grinned.

'Sorry,' I said.

'Liberty Hall.'

'Sorry,' I said again.

'Tom.' James crept close to Tom. 'We've found out all the animals can talk.'

Tom Foley groaned and lay back, covering his face with his hat.

'Tom, we messed up the otter hunt and we want you to help us mess up other hunts and badger baiting and shooting.'

'That's war on respectability.' Tom spoke from under his hat.

'Just up your street,' said Joker.

'You leave my street alone,' said Tom from under his hat.

'We need your help and your car,' said Andrew.

'My car.' Tom Foley sat up again.

'Yes, if your girl friend will join us,' I said, feeling rather wily.

'Who is your girl friend?' Andrew could be fearfully clumsy.

Tom Foley began to laugh rather like the woodpecker. 'Oh, my girl friend,' he said, wiping a hand across his eyes. 'My girl friend,' and he laughed again. 'This is my girl friend.' His encircling arm closed tighter round the little dog. 'Floss,' said Tom Foley. The little dog's expression changed entirely as she looked into his face and her bushy tail moved.

'Can you speak too, Floss?'

'Yes,' said Floss.

Andrew told Tom Foley about Mr Bull, the mouse, the birds, the other animals and the result of the otter hunt. Tom Foley and Floss listened. Andrew finished and we all looked at Tom.

'Well?' said Tom.

'We thought you might help us,' I said.

'Did you?'

'We thought with your car and carrier pigeons you would like to help,' said Angela.

'They are not carrier pigeons, they are ordinary wood pigeons.' Tom Foley showed his teeth in a slight smile.

'Oh,' Angela looked taken aback.

Tom Foley appeared to relent. 'You *might* call them carrier pigeons if you stretched a point.'

'What point?' said James.

'I've taken their rings off. They have retired, so to speak.'

Somewhere in the wood a pigeon began to coo drowsily.

'They don't like the long train journeys in baskets, see. So they retire.'

'And you help them,' Angela said quickly.

'Yes.'

'We want to help more than otters and pigeons. Think of badgers,' Andrew said.

'Ah well, badgers. As you can see, I'm more or less a lodger among the badgers. Go find a badger, Floss.'

Floss left Tom Foley and trotted to the nearest set and went down it.

Tom looked at us. 'Fond of badgers?' he asked.

'They are marvellous,' said Andrew. 'They do nobody any harm. They are terribly clever and civilized and people dig them out and torture them. It's disgusting what people do to badgers.'

'What about cows, sheep, pigs and the like?' Tom queried.

'That's awful too, but they are not persecuted for sport.'

'No.'

Behind us a huge badger heaved itself silently out of one of the largest sets followed by Floss.

'What's going on, and in daylight too?' said the badger. 'I can't see a thing.'

'Well, old man, these children have found out you can all speak and they want to help you, stop you being tormented, and other animals too, for sporting reasons.'

The badger blinked in the sun and we admired his wonderful markings.

'Nobody ever comes here,' said the badger.

'They might,' I said.

'They mucked up an otter hunt this morning and they want to save the foxes and deer and so on as well as you.'

'Foxes eat sheep and chickens.' The badger looked doubtful.

'Not always,' I said.

'Need a lot of organizing. I'm sleepy,' said the badger.

'Were the otters pleased and grateful?' There was a trace of malice in Tom's voice.

'No, not at all. They thought we were interfering,' said Angela.

'Can't expect them to like you all of a sudden,' said Floss, in a rather high whining voice. 'I don't,' she added, with a sidelong look at Blueprint.

'With your car, Tom, we could travel long distances and give the animals warning,' said James. 'It's a beautiful car,' he added.

'And your pigeons can travel great distances,' said Angela. 'Once the animals know, we could just send them messages and they could cover their tracks and hide, or something,' she added lamely.

'This great wood could become a sanctuary,' I said, suddenly inspired. 'As it's meant to be.'

'It's going to cost money and make a lot of work,' said Tom.

'Surely it's worth it?' Angela looked frustrated. 'Think of all the things we could do without money.'

'Such as?' said Andrew.

'Teaching trout not to rise to a fly and foxes not to worry lambs. They hardly ever do anyway.'

'What about cats and mice? What about me and rabbits? What about squirrels eating pigeon's eggs?' Floss whined and snarled.

'Oh, you are all so difficult,' exclaimed James.

'It's a difficult subject,' said the badger.

'But will you help?' I said.

There was a long pause.

'Tell you what, we will think about it.' Tom Foley put his hat over his eyes again and lay back. Floss curled herself against his side and watched us.

'A lot of thinking is needed, not just enthusiasm,' said the badger.

'May we come again?' Andrew's voice was disappointed and sad.

'Oh yes, any time.' The badger left us.

We all felt tremendously let down.

Floss was looking at us with her beady eyes.

'The car has no petrol.' She made the statement flatly.

'Would it help if it had?'

'Certainly.'

'Would you?'

Floss grinned. 'Certainly.'

'So it boils down to money!' exclaimed James.

'Yes,' said Floss.

'Nonsense!' Tom spoke unexpectedly from under his hat. 'There is a lot can be done without money, though if we use the car we have to have petrol and oil.'

'Oh, Tom!'

Our hearts leapt.

'Oh, Tom, you are marvellous!' Angela sprang to her feet.

'We need the foxes' help badly,' I said.

'There's been a vixen sitting behind you ever since you came, listening.'

'Why didn't the dogs let us know?'

'They know, but don't know whether you should know.' The voice from under the hat was lazy and sleepy.

'Why doesn't she come forward?' Andrew sounded rather pompous.

'Would you if you'd fed your family on a Johnson lamb for several days?' Tom's voice trailed off into a gentle snore under the hat.

'Oh, dear, how complicated it all is,' I said.

Floss looked at me with a sneer and, lying close to Tom, closed her eyes.

'That lamb was a weakling. My father said so,' said James. 'He said the foxes were welcome to it if they didn't make a habit of it.'

'He isn't like most farmers,' a thin, high voice said behind us. 'He is odd.'

'What do you mean, odd?' James turned with the rest of us and stared up the bank to where we could just discern a vixen sitting upright in the shade.

'Well, odd,' said the vixen, 'very odd. He cares when he sells a cow. He loves his sheep. He dotes on his pigs.'

'He says the most awful things to them,' James muttered.

'That's just to hide his feelings. You see, pigs are bright and there is nothing you can do with a pig except eat it. You can't milk it as you do a cow and let it have a reasonably long life, or shear it as you do a sheep for its wool, and sheep have quite long lives too.'

'Except when they are eaten,' said Andrew.

'Oh well,' said the vixen, 'you can't have everything.' She, too, yawned and disappeared in the shadows of the trees.

'All yawning and going to sleep.' Andrew got up. 'We must find the money for petrol and oil for Tom's car.'

'That will take years,' James grumbled. 'Where is the car anyway?'

'In the quarry.' Floss spoke without opening her eyes.

'Would he mind if we looked at it?' James stood up and I joined him.

'Not if you cover it up again,' Tom murmured from under his hat.

'Goodbye,' we said, but no one answered and we followed Joker and Blueprint down the hill.

Shadowed by trees and covered by a groundsheet, Tom's car was parked in a corner of the quarry. No one would have noticed it if they had not known it was there. We lifted the groundsheet and looked at it with admiration.

'A 1924 Bullnose,' said James.

'But hardly any petrol,' said Andrew, looking into the tank.

The Johnson boys and Angela and I had for a long time made merry over what we called our parents' daily moan when the post arrived. 'Bills!' they would cry. 'Nothing but bills. It is high time you children grew up and earned your living.'

Now it was for us to moan, worry and fret over money, and ponder over ways and means to collect enough to run Tom's car. We walked about frowning and scuffling our shoes as we walked, kicking stones ill-temperedly. The days passed and we grumbled. Between us we raised seventeen and eleven from our pocket money, which we put in a jar in a hole in the wood.

We shared our troubles with the animals and birds.

'Money has never worried me,' said Mr Bull, crunching his seed in his strong beak. 'Not so long as I get my food.'

'Money,' said the cow Mr Johnson was selling to the Master of the Otter Hounds. 'Money is going to change hands but I shan't see it. It only goes towards paying the vet.'

'Money,' said the mouse. 'We have some money.' And he and several other mice kindly rolled two shilling pieces, a threepenny bit and a halfpenny out of their hole by the electric light plug. That brought our hoard up to a pound and twopence-halfpenny. We thanked the mice.

Early one morning Angela came into my room. 'Somebody has left a huge sea-trout at the back door,' she said.

'That's the otters,' said Mr Bull. 'Sell it.'

Angela smoothed over the otter's teeth marks and sold the fish at the hotel. The owner gave her fifteen shillings. That brought us up to one pound, fifteen and twopence-halfpenny, and we went to thank the otters but they were all out.

'Can't leave a note because they can't read,' I said.

'What can we do?' said Angela. 'What can we do to get more money?'

'I think we should ask the animals. It's no good asking Tom Foley because he spends everything he earns on drink and Floss doesn't stop him because she likes beer.'

We knew this to be true because my father had told my mother that he had seen Tom Foley pour beer into a saucer in the pub and Floss drink it.

'If we got enough we could run the car,' said Andrew.

'I will ask Floss,' said Joker, who was very fond of visiting Floss when he could slip away from the farm.

'It is time I took a hand in this,' said Vice. 'I shall speak to the dogs.'

We looked doubtfully at Vice, who had recently caught a mouse.

'This needs brains,' said Vice.

'It's terrible. The otter hounds keep meeting and in August they will start deer hunting and the cubbing begins.'

'All the rich men are fishing now,' said Vice, gazing ahead of him into infinity.

'We warn the fish.'

'That's not what I meant.'

'The otters don't care for the fish to be warned,' I said. 'It was good of them to bring us that sea-trout.'

'I should have liked it,' said Vice.

'Vice, you get more than enough to eat.' Angela, quite rightly I felt, did not think Vice was wholeheartedly on our side.

'I'll talk to the dogs all the same.' Vice went to the door and miaowed as though he could not talk at all. We looked at each other and sighed.

'Let's go and ask for more pocket money,' said Angela.

'It won't do any good,' said Mr Bull. 'Dash it, even birdseed has gone up.'

'Then logically pocket money should go up too.' Angela twanged one of the bars of Mr Bull's cage.

We went to look for our parents, who were sitting in the sun in the garden. As we approached them we heard my mother say: 'I hate you letting the fishing, darling, you so enjoy it.'

'A hundred pounds a month is not to be sneezed at. Johnson has let his. The girls have to be educated and both Johnson and I have had the best of the river, May and June. Besides – ' my father was dreamily watching Blueprint running after Vice into the wood, 'the fish simply are not rising this year.'

'Then it seems dishonest to let.'

'Not really. There are plenty of fish. These chaps may catch them. They have money to throw about. They may be lucky.'

'It doesn't seem honest to me,' said my mother.

'I told them,' said my father, 'but there it is. Fishing is hard to get. They are staying at the hotel. They said they were given a very good sea-trout their first evening there. I wonder where it came from. I'd bet anything we had otters nearby but I never see them.'

'There are no otters round here,' said my mother.

'None at all,' said Angela.

'What do you girls want?' asked my father abruptly.

'More pocket money,' I said.

'No!' my father shouted.

'What next!' exclaimed my mother.

Our father went crossly into the house.

'Who has he let the fishing to?' I asked tactfully.

'Oh, he and Mr Johnson have let the whole two miles they have between them to some men called Macintosh or Jersey or Raglan or some name like that. They are from London.'

'Cardigan,' said Angela, who was rather good at names. 'They are publishers, rather "avant garde".'

'When are they starting to fish?'

'Tonight, I believe. D'you know what "avant garde" means, Angela?'

Angela shook her head, laughing.

We went down the river into the wood. By the otters' holt I called: 'Otters!'

There was a sort of whispering inside. 'What is it now?' said one of the baby otters irritably.

'Our father and Mr Johnson have let the fishing to two city gents.'

'Oh, have they?'

'Keep out of their way, won't you?'

'Don't be daft,' another otter answered.

Blueprint joined us, wagging his tail. 'Just had a word with Vice and Joker,' he said. 'Joker is going to tell Floss. She will help.'

'Help at what?' Blueprint was looking too amused to be safe.

'Oh, never mind,' he said. My father whistled and Blueprint went tearing off, his ears laid back.

We spent the evening watching the two visitors casting their lines. Now and again a fish rose with a swish and plopped back into the water.

'There are lots of fish but they just don't seem to be taking,' said one Mr Cardigan to the other as they passed us.

'Try again early tomorrow,' said the second Mr Cardigan.

'Try away,' said Angela, as we went off to school the next day and saw the two men getting out their rods near the bridge.

When we got home we heard voices in our house and went in to find both the Mr Cardigans talking to my mother.

'Oh, hullo darlings,' said our mother.

'Hullo,' we said, and then 'How do you do?' to the two Mr Cardigans.

'I should ring the police if I were you,' my mother said to the Mr Cardigans.

'We only wondered if you had seen anybody,' said one Mr Cardigan. 'We were watching the river.'

'What's happened?' asked Angela. 'A nice murder?'

'No. Mr Cardigan and his brother have both had money stolen from their wallets which they left in their coats while they were fishing. The wallets were there but no money.'

'How odd,' I said.

'How much?' asked Angela.

'About forty pounds, between us.'

'Forty pounds!' My voice squeaked in astonishment. 'Are you the sort of people who carry forty pounds on your persons?'

'Don't be rude, Kate,' said my mother. 'You should certainly tell the police,' she said to the older Mr Cardigan, 'and we will get hold of my husband when he comes in. He is a solicitor.'

'He's hardly likely to have pinched it,' said Angela. 'Who has been up and down the river, mother?'

'Nobody,' said my mother. 'I've been here all day.'

'It's very queer,' I said.

'Go and wash before tea,' said my mother, who never remembered to say things like that unless there were people visiting. 'You will stay to tea, won't you?' she said to the Mr Cardigans. 'After all, it's our land you were robbed on.'

'What a drama!' said Angela as she walked upstairs, ran the water over her hands in the bathroom and wiped the dirt off on to a towel. 'What a lovely drama!'

We had tea. My father came in. He took the two Cardigans off to the police. The police came in a squad car and tramped up and down the wood by the river. The Johnson boys and Joker came with us, and my mother and father, and Mr Johnson when he had finished milking. We all crashed about a bit in the wood. The two policemen looked very wise and went away and finally we went to bed.

When the house was quiet Angela came into my room with Blueprint and Vice. 'Fancy us having the police,' she said.

'Yes, fancy,' said Vice.

'What do you mean – "Fancy" – in that tone of voice?' I asked.

'Only fancy,' said Vice, who was sitting staring at Mr Bull.

'Stop staring at Mr Bull,' I said.

'Oh-ho-ho-ho-ho!' Blueprint lay on his back, switching himself from side to side his eyes rolling.

'What's the "ho-ho" for?' asked Angela.

Mr Bull gave a cheerful pipe and Vice began licking his white stomach. We could hear his harsh tongue scraping through his soft fur.

'Forty quid,' said Mr Bull.

'We all know they think they lost forty quid,' said Angela. 'The police don't think so, nor does father. You could see by their faces they didn't believe the Cardigans.'

'But we've got forty quid,' said Vice.

'We have,' growled Blueprint.

'Who took it?' I said.

'Joker and Floss and I,' said Blueprint.

Angela laughed. 'Where is it?'

'Down the mousehole. Now you can buy all the petrol you want.'

8

'I have asked the Cardigans to tea,' said my mother at breakfast. 'It's high time the girls met some respectable people.'

'Oh,' said my father. 'Er – I suppose it is.'

'It's terrible that they should be robbed on our land,' my mother continued, eating her breakfast. 'Not that I like the police tramping about the wood in the nesting season.'

'No,' said my father. 'Only doing their job,' he added.

'They long for a bit of crime.' I helped myself to a banana.

'You know,' I said to Angela as we walked down the road to meet Mrs Johnson and the boys, 'stealing is a crime.'

'In a good cause.' Angela began to run, seeing Mrs Johnson bring her car to a halt at the corner. 'Besides,' she added, 'we can't get at it, it's down the mousehole.'

'What's down the mousehole?' said Mrs Johnson as we climbed into her car.

'Only an old marble.'

'They always find their way to mouseholes. It's most peculiar. I think they play.' Mrs Johnson drove rather recklessly along the road. 'I must leave a message at the pub,' she said.

'Who for?' said Angela.

'Tom Foley. We want to pay him what we owe him for the lambing. We never know where to find him except the pub.' Mrs Johnson stopped at the pub and Andrew went into the ironmongers'.

'What's he doing?' asked Angela.

'Buying a can.' James had a harassed look. 'We shall be late. A can for petrol.'

Andrew came out and got in beside his mother. 'Did you leave a message?' He carried a jerry can.

'Yes. They say they will tell him when they see him.'

Mrs Johnson drove off. I watched our local milk lorry hurtling towards us. We passed it with a narrow margin and Mrs Johnson looked pleased, though the lorry driver didn't.

James and I did rather well at school that day. We had a system of helping each other. He did the maths and science and I did the history, geography and anything else I knew about. He was very good at copying my handwriting. Andrew and Angela did the same thing in their form.

Driving home the two boys sat in the back and whispered with Angela. I didn't like this as I like to know what's going on. Outside our front door two rods were propped.

'The Cardigans!' Angela loathed visitors.

'I'd forgotten.' I looked at the beautiful fibre-glass rods and smart bags and creels.

'Ah, here you are,' said my mother. We shook hands.

'Found your money yet?' Angela was a born criminal.

'No, we haven't.' The elder Mr Cardigan spoke from a nice Queen Anne chair which Vice likes scratching.

'We have done the same thing before.'

'The same what?' My mother's hand was trembling with the weight of the teapot as she began pouring tea.

'We are old bachelors,' said the younger Mr Cardigan. 'We have lived together for so many years that very often either both of us do a thing or neither of us does it.'

'What's that to do with losing forty pounds?' Angela passed a plate of buns to the older Mr Cardigan.

'I can see you are a lawyer's daughter.' The older Mr Cardigan politely refused a bun. 'You see, we both think we cashed cheques.'

Our mother raised her eyebrows.

'If you are not careful you will both be paying our father and Mr Johnson for the fishing twice.' Angela took two buns and, forgetting to pass them to me, ate ferociously.

'Oh, your father and Mr Johnson would tell us. Anyone in this delightful place would.' The younger Mr Cardigan smiled winningly at Angela, who could not smile back because her mouth was full, and we did know that a mouth full of half-chewed bun isn't attractive.

'Cash down,' I murmured. The younger Mr Cardigan looked at me and quickly looked away.

'Well, we must be going,' said the fatter Mr Cardigan and they got up and thanked our mother very politely and collected their fishing tackle and went off down the stream, speaking quietly about the evening rise.

We helped our mother clear up tea.

Angela said: 'They pay in cash.'

'What do you mean?' I said.

'Evasion of income tax, stupid. They pay cash for everything.'

'Oh,' I said, 'How did you guess?'

'They don't want enquiries made and the police with their great boots and notebooks tramping round. They paid Mr Johnson in cash.

'Did they?'

'Andrew told me.'

'What about father?'

'They will give him a cheque because he is a lawyer.'

'I think you girls have very nasty minds,' said my mother.

'Well, they have paid the hotel cash in advance.'

'How do you know these things?' Our mother looked genuinely astonished.

'The hotel told me,' said Angela patiently. 'They were awfully pleased.'

Our mother hung the tea towel on the hook and left the room.

'Did they tell you when you sold them the sea-trout?' I asked.

'Yes. Nobody is really honest.'

'Hm,' I said and went up to my room where Vice was sitting watching the mousehole.

'Don't do that, Vice.'

'I must,' said Vice.

'Why?'

'If I go away they are quite capable of chewing up the money and making nests of it.'

'I feel terrible being party to a robbery,' I said.

'Rubbish,' said Vice.

'Don't be a hypocrite,' said Mr Bull.

I went and looked out of the window. I could see Blueprint and Angela walking down the fisherman's path. I stood watching the light slanting through the trees and listening to the birds and the monotonous screech, wind-in, screech, as the two Cardigans fished slowly down the river. Presently Angela and Andrew came out of the wood together, laughing. Andrew was carrying an open envelope in one hand.

'Now we need the cash,' he said as they came in.

'Come away from the hole, Vice.' Angela picked Vice up tenderly in her arms. 'Tell the mouse to shove up the money,' she said cajolingly. Vice purred and put up a soft paw to her face.

'Hurry up,' said Mr Bull.

There was a rustling sound and a five pound note came out of the hole.

'We need much more than that,' said Andrew.

We all watched as note after note appeared through the hole. Andrew counted them, put them into the envelope and licked it up.

'Oh,' I said. 'Petrol galore!'

'There is another one pound ten in the hole,' said Mr Bull.

'Shove it up,' said Vice in a nasty voice.

'Bedding,' a mouse said, just out of reach in the wainscot.

'Give them some paper,' said Mr Bull.

'But the thread would so amuse the children.'

'Shove it up,' said Vice again.

The last pound and ten shilling note came through the hole and I put two rolled sheets of writing paper down in exchange.

'Call a swallow,' said Andrew to Mr Bull.

Mr Bull piped several times and a swallow swooped near the sill and snatched the two notes from between Andrew's fingers.

'Why the swallows?' said Angela.

'Taking them to Floss.' Andrew tickled Blueprint under the chin so that he closed his eyes in ecstacy. 'Now Floss and Tom can go to the pub tonight and fill up the car.'

'Drinking is so vulgar,' said Vice.

'Some people call it an art,' Mr Bull piped.

'I think I shall go out for a while.' Vice slid through the door and was gone. We watched him slip into the wood and saw our mother make a dash to catch him. She came back alone, looking rather flushed.

'Do you think?' I said.

'Yes,' said Andrew.

'Do something, Mr Bull.'

Mr Bull piped a few times and the sound of the birds' songs changed into high scolding notes as warnings were carried down through the wood.

'Vice!' said Angela.

'Don't be silly.' Mr Bull was crunching seeds. 'You children are party to theft. Only I am innocent.'

Angela twanged a bar of his cage twice.

9

We went down to the Johnsons' farm to pick up James. We met Vice wandering up the path, his eyes wide and innocent and his tail in the air. He passed us, but we were used to rudeness from cats.

'Your father will be struck off the Rolls,' Vice leered over his shoulder.

'He drives a Ford,' James said.

'*Legal* Rolls.' Angela was aghast. 'We must give it back. All that lovely lolly – Blueprint, we must get the money back and post it to the Hotel.' Angela was almost crying.

'I'll do it tonight.' Blueprint spoke comfortingly and Angela sighed with relief.

At the Johnsons' bridge we sat astride the parapet and watched the two Mr Cardigans.

'One of them slipped and filled his waders,' said James.

'Too bad,' said Andrew. 'We are going over the hill to the Broughtons' land.'

'Why?'

'To look at the game larder.'

'It's beastly,' said James, and added, 'Joker is busy with father.'

We looked away up the hillside and saw a flock of sheep moving reluctantly towards an open gate and Joker running silently to and fro behind them, his head and tail down and ears attentive to Mr Johnson's whistle.

'I shall escort you,' said Blueprint, who feels rather bad sometimes about having no exact profession.

We walked quickly up the hill. It was beautiful land, but ruined for us because the Broughtons let it all for shooting and the syndicate who rented the shoot employed two gamekeepers. At the top of the hill we lay down in a row and watched.

'Feeding time,' I said.

One of the gamekeepers came out of his cottage carrying a bucket. Behind him trotted a labrador.

'I must get at him,' grumbled Blueprint. 'Or Floss would do it better.'

We watched the keeper walk slowly to the edge of the corn and call 'Cluck, cluck, cluck.' Out of the corn came a stream of pheasants, high-stepping cocks and elegant hens. The keeper scattered corn liberally and the pheasants pecked and ate. The keeper watched them eat and seemed to be counting them. Leaving the edge of the wood, he walked along the cornfield scattering grain, glancing behind him to see the partridges sneak out of the corn and start eating. We trotted quickly downhill to the back of the cottage.

'I shall go and tell that dog we are visiting.' Blueprint scampered away from us.

Behind the cottage we came to two long wire lines tied between trees. In different stages of decay there hung from these wires the corpses of stoats, weasels, squirrels, carrion crows, jays and magpies. The smell was horrible.

Blueprint rejoined us and said: 'He takes an hour over his tea and then goes round the traps.'

A tiny voice remarked: 'That's my mate, third from the left.' Third from the left a slip of fur hung greasy with rot. A weasel showed itself for a moment.

'Move over to the big wood,' said James.

'But there is such good eating here,' answered the weasel.

'We want to help you,' I said.

'So I hear.' The weasel disappeared.

'It's hardly likely to trust us, is it?' said Angela. 'Come on.' She led the way at a run.

'You help, Blueprint,' said James, and Blueprint dashed ahead.

'He can find the traps,' I said.

'They are illegal,' said Angela.

'You are a fine one to talk.'

Ahead of us we heard a muffled yelp and we ran towards it. We found Blueprint standing waiting for us with an expression of shame on his face, his paw firmly held in a gin trap.

'You clot!' said Andrew, releasing him.

'Are you hurt?' I asked.

'Not much.' Blueprint licked the paw while Angela examined it.

'Come on, there must be a whole line of them.' James trotted ahead and we heard him give an exclamation of pleasure as he sprang a trap. Walking cautiously, with Blueprint limping behind us, we found a long line of traps and sprang them by poking a stick at them. In the last we found a dead rabbit and left it.

'As foolish as you, Blueprint.' Andrew looked at the rabbit.

'Don't go on about it.' Blueprint looked hurt.

'Where are the bird traps?' I asked.

'At the very edge of the wood where the pheasants are fed.'

We turned back. The bird traps were also in a long line and each held its complement of grain-eating birds. We let them out.

'Watch out.' Blueprint crouched down and we all lay on our stomachs in the fern and listened. Through the wood we could hear footsteps and voices.

'Not a thing in the big traps,' said a voice. 'Just one rabbit.'

'Don't get much these days,' another voice answered. 'Myxomatosis has done for most of them. This one's empty. Funny. And all the seed has gone.'

'Gone from this one too. Can't make it out.'

'They seem all right.'

The labrador came and muttered something to Blueprint and then ran off.

'He says we should go now before they see us,' said Blueprint importantly.

'I'm thinking of writing a dictionary of oaths.' Andrew was listening to the gamekeepers with a beatific expression. 'I took the petrol to Tom. The car's ready.' A pair of foxes trotted together towards the Broughton shoot.

'Traps,' called James.

The foxes leered and trotted on. 'Don't worry us,' one said.

We came home through the village. The pub door was open and we heard voices rumbling and occasional laughter. Tom Foley, with Mr Johnson's hat on the back of his head, was standing with his back to us. At his feet sat Floss. We saw the landlord pass a saucer to Tom, who filled it and laid it down in front of Floss. Floss drank, lapping slowly. I had the impression that she could see us, but when the saucer was empty she deliberately turned her back, leapt on to the stool beside Tom and leant her chin on the bar. We said goodnight to the boys. Vice met us in the hall. 'You might at least have brought me the rabbit,' he said.

'How do you know so soon?' whispered Angela.

'Owls and otters pass the news.'

'Have you heard too, Mr Bull?' I combed my hair, which was full of bits of bracken, before going down to supper.

'Naturally.'

'We must warn all those pheasants and partridges that they are going to be shot,' I said.

'They are rather annoyed about you letting all the trapped birds go.'

'What?' I said.

'Well, they eat their corn.'

From my sleep I was wakened by a persistent tickling at my nose. I sneezed. A tiny voice squeaked: 'Don't do that.' The mouse came back near my face. 'You awake?' it said.

'Yes.'

'We've made a nice nest. The wife is very pleased.'

'You didn't wake her up to tell her that.' Mr Bull spoke rather nastily from under the cover of his cage.

'Well, in the summer we go down to the garden at night with the children and meet our cousins. It's a bit of a risk because of the owls, but we keep in the shelter of the plants.' The mouse clutched the sheet near my face, thinking of the owls.

'Go on. Get to the point.'

'Well, tonight the otters told us cubbing starts next week. The pigs told them.'

'What pigs?'

'Mr Johnson's pigs.'

I thought of the Johnsons' pigs – huge elephantine sows who each lived in a little wooden hut with a corrugated iron roof in a field.

'Why should the pigs mind?' I was now fully awake.

'Five of them are due to farrow next week. Hounds disturb them.' The mouse scrambled off my bed and scratched its way down the bedclothes.

'Time you did something sharpish,' said Mr Bull. I got up and went into Angela's room. Blueprint, lying on the greater part of the bed with his head on the pillow, thumped his tail. Vice, curled in a ball at Angela's feet, opened his green eyes.

'Aahh,' Angela groaned. 'What do you want?' She was lying straight on the very edge of the bed so that Vice and Blueprint should be comfortable.

'Wake up. The mouse says the pigs know that cubbing is starting next week.'

'The pigs?'

'That's what he said.'

'Action!' exclaimed Angela.

'When?' said Blueprint.

'At once,' said Angela. 'We will let you out now and you can go and tell Floss and Joker. Vice, you must go too.'

'Oh, not now.' Vice curled himself into a tighter ball and shut his eyes.

'Yes, now.'

Vice gave Angela a very nasty look and shut his eyes again.

'Go on, Vice,' I said in a wheedling tone.

Vice got up and arched his back, clawed at the bedclothes several times, and yawned.

'Let us out.' Blueprint trotted to the door. We opened the front door and they went out into the night.

'Mr Bull,' said Angela.

'Oh, not *again*.' Mr Bull woke up crossly.

'Mr Bull, will you warn all the birds as soon as it's light?'

'All right, but let me sleep now.'

'Tomorrow we must all go and see Tom Foley.' Angela went back to bed.

The mouse was wandering about my bedroom floor. 'Got any cotton wool?' he said. 'It makes a good lining for the nest.' I rummaged in my dressing-table drawer and found a bit which had been in the top of a Disprin bottle. The mouse pulled it into his hole. I went back to sleep, and at first light Mr Bull began to pipe loudly and the birds in the garden answered in a loud chorus.

When after breakfast we went down to the Johnsons' farm, we saw James crawling backwards out of one of the sows' little huts. He was laughing.

'Don't disturb those sows, you fool!' shouted Mr Johnson. One of the sows came grunting up to him. 'Peace and quiet is what you want.' Mr Johnson scraped a stick along the sow's side so that she closed her tiny eyes with pleasure and twisted her body with joy.

'They won't get any peace and quiet next week,' said Angela. 'Cubbing is starting on Saturday.'

'Not on my land it isn't.' The boys' father stopped scratching the sow. 'Five of these beauties are having families at any minute. I'm not having a lot of hounds and idiot fools riding over my land disturbing my pigs.'

'Tell the hunt then,' said Andrew.

'I might,' said Mr Johnson. 'Anyone seen Joker? I need him for the sheep.'

'No,' we said, and all four of us walked away into the woods.

We met Joker trotting towards us. 'Fixed the car?' he enquired.

'Yes.'

'Must go back, alas, to work.' Joker passed us and ran fast back to the farm.

'Joker is conscientious,' said Andrew.

We walked to the clearing and here, as before, lay Tom Foley and Floss. 'Don't disturb,' said Floss, baring her teeth. 'Bad enough having Joker and Blueprint.'

'What's the news, Blueprint?' Andrew pulled a bag of sweets from his pocket and handed them round.

'Can't wake Tom.' Blueprint crunched the sweet and looked as though he could do with another.

'I'm awake.' Tom spoke with his eyes shut.

'Tom, the hounds are starting cubbing next Saturday.'

'Well?'

'We must warn all the foxes.'

'Warning doesn't do much good.' Tom Foley still kept his eyes shut. 'Need somebody with a gift for organization.' He seemed to drift off to sleep again, and Floss coolly closed her eyes and put her nose under her tail. James trotted across the clearing and looked under a bush, and then stretched his arm into the lower branches. Tom Foley sat up.

'What's going on?'

'I was going to give you some Alka-Selzer.'

'Good idea.' Tom Foley caressed Floss, who snuggled up to him. James filled a mug with water and added two Alka-Selzer tablets and handed it to Tom, who drank, making a face, and then burped.

'Now what's all this about?' Tom Foley looked at us down his long nose.'

'We need you and your car and a lot of advice.'

'Badgers.' Tom was sitting up.

'Oh, we are listening,' a badger remarked from a set.

'What do you advise?' Blueprint spoke respectfully.

'The foxes must be told to come here and Tom can bring the smallest in his car. We don't mind lodging them for the day.' The badger came out into the open and blinked in the bright light.

'How do I collect them?' Tom seemed quite agreeable to the arrangement.

'I shall go with you and tell you where to stop.' The vixen we had met before spoke from a clump of bracken.

'That's all very well, but we don't want the hounds all over this wood all day. They will be a damn nuisance.' Tom Foley lay back again.

Floss raised herself and began talking into Tom's ear. He listened and then let out a shout of laughter.

'What did she say?' Blueprint gazed longingly at Floss.

'Floss will take care of the hounds while we take care of the foxes.'

'All those huge hounds?' Blueprint looked both jealous and shocked.

'Just that.' Tom was still laughing. 'Anyone knows any horses?' he added.

'I do,' said Angela unexpectedly. 'I belong to the Pony Club.'

'Good Lord, so you do!' said Andrew.

'You'd better join in the hunt then,' said Floss nastily.

'What do you ride?' asked the vixen.

'Old Bodkin's horse.'

'Oh, I know *him*.' There was a wealth of relief and meaning in the vixen's voice.

'Then that's settled.' Tom Foley lay back, covered his face with his hat and breathed deeply. The vixen had come very close to James. 'I don't mind you,' she said craftily.

'The pigs have volunteered,' said James slyly. 'One of those sows is a Holy Terror.'

'Even with my father,' said Andrew.

'Old Bodkin's horse and Floss will see to it that the hunting people enjoy themselves.' Tom Foley spoke sleepily.

'I wonder how.' Angela looked uneasy. Floss opened her eyes and gave her a long appraising look.

'There may be some unexpected allies.' The badger turned and went back into the depths of the ground. On my way home I leant into the otters' holt and told them the news. I did not see them but I heard laughter.

⚜ 11 ⚜

'I say, Mr Bodkin.' Angela and I leant on the gate beside Mr Bodkin. 'Will you lend me your horse next Saturday?'

Mr Bodkin, who was a long thin man with a sad face, stroked the horse's head between its eyes as the horse nibbled with blue-gray lips at his coat.

'No,' said Mr Bodkin. 'I'm riding him myself. You can ride that thing.' He pointed towards a thin, racy animal standing twenty yards away, her ears pricked and a look of nervous horror on her face.

'When did you get her?' Angela looked away from Mr Bodkin's tranquil horse to the bundle of nerves staring at us.

'Bought that cheap. She's unrideable. Uncatchable too. Catch her and you can ride her.'

'What on earth made you buy her?' I asked.

'She's pretty. Well bred too. Make a lovely child's pony.' Mr Bodkin spoke in jerks.

'But uncatchable,' said Angela.

'Yes, I was had, I was.'

'I suppose she bucks, kicks, rears, runs away with you and bites.'

'She'll get you off under a branch or against a gatepost,' admitted Mr Bodkin. 'You school her for me and I'll lend her to you for the Shows and the hunting.'

'Thanks,' said Angela ungratefully.

Mr Bodkin wandered away. The quiet horse nuzzled us over the gate while the nervous new mare snorted and blew down her nose. Angela climbed over the gate and the new horse broke into a wild ungainly gallop up the field, throwing out her legs and tossing her head. Blueprint, the old horse and I waited.

'I hear there's goings-on,' said the quiet horse. 'I like hunting myself.'

'It's unfair.' Blueprint sat beside me watching Angela who, reaching the middle of the field, sat down. We could see she was talking, the new horse stood twenty yards away from her with its back turned and ears laid back. After what seemed a long time the horse turned round and, walking slowly and edgily, tiptoed up to Angela and began nibbling her hair. Angela did not move but went on talking. Presently she stood up and she and the horse seemed to confront each other. Suddenly the horse gave a loud whinnying laugh.

'You see,' we heard Angela say as she walked back with the horse to the gate, 'I won't frighten you if you don't frighten me.'

'I shall just pretend then,' said the horse.

'Make a good show,' said the quiet horse.

'I'll make a show all right,' said the nervous horse.

'Don't overdo it. I hate falling off,' said Angela.

We heard both horses whinnying as we walked home.

'Made an arrangement?' asked Blueprint.

'Yes,' said Angela. 'There are no flies on that horse.'

'Circus act?' enquired Blueprint, who had seen many circuses on television.

'Yes.' Angela looked thoughtful.

We went into our house and saw our mother putting the telephone back in its cradle. 'Awkward for your father,' she said.

'What is?'

'The Broughton syndicate don't want the hounds going over their land. Your father acts for them.'

'The keepers shoot foxes,' I said.

'It's very awkward,' repeated my mother. 'Are you going out on Saturday, Angela?'

'Yes,' said Angela with a boot face.

'Pity you don't ride,' said my mother to me. 'You get to know such nice people.'

'Such as?' I asked rather rudely.

'Oh, all the hunting people and the Pony Club and, well, everybody.'

'All your friends?' asked Angela.

'Well, not exactly, but you know what I mean, darling.'

'Come to the Meet then on Saturday.'

'I might. But they disturb the birds,' my mother said weakly.

'What about the foxes?'

'They disturb the birds too. But the hunting people are – '

'Crashing bores,' I said.

'I'm a hunting person,' said Angela, twisting a short piece of my hair near my neck. I hit her.

'Now, girls,' said my mother.

'Little birds in their nests should agree.' Mr Johnson came into the house without knocking, with bits of mud slipping off his gumboots on to our clean hall floor. Joker came behind him and Blueprint let out a ferocious bark and hurled himself at him. In the narrow confines of the hall the dogs made a fearful noise, snapping, snarling and bashing to and fro. Mr Johnson shouted and we separated them.

'They never hurt each other,' said Mr Johnson.

'No, they don't,' said my mother. 'What can I do for you?'

'It's my pigs, really. Do you think we can ask the hunt to keep off my land until they have farrowed?'

'No.' My mother was looking crossly at the mud now well ground into the hall carpet by the dog fight. 'No, there is nothing we can do. Besides, your Betty is more than a match for any pack of hounds.'

'Yes. I'll station her near the pigs next week, then it won't look like me. I'm selling to the Master. I don't want to offend him. He is buying my hay.'

'Moral coward.' Our mother laughed and Angela grinned.

I felt something was going on which I didn't understand. Angela for a moment had looked like Floss.

I went up to see Mr Bull. 'Do you want to go out?' I asked.

'No, I don't trust Vice.'

'In this world everyone is afraid of someone,' said Vice.

'I suppose so.'

'I hear on the grapevine that Angela is going hunting.'

'Very brave of her,' I said loyally.

'Hope she enjoys it.' Vice began staring at Mr Bull.

'Stop it, Vice.'

Angela rode Mr Bodkin's new mare slowly and sedately round Mr Bodkin's field. She got off when she saw me. 'Everything is going to be all right on Saturday.' She took off the saddle and bridle and said to the horse: 'Show Kate what you can do.' The horse lashed out with both hind feet and kicked the gate with a clang. Then she reared up on end and, dropping on all four feet, did a series of ghastly twisting bucks. Then she dashed under a low branch of a tree and came back to us with her ears back, her eyes rolling and teeth bared.

'Very funny,' said the old horse sarcastically.

'Only a child murderer would buy you,' I said to the horse.

The horse looked smugly from under long lashes.

'Come on,' said Angela. 'There isn't really much time.' We went back to Mr Bull. On the way Tom Foley passed us in his old Morris, wearing Mr Johnson's hat. He waved but Floss, sitting beside him, didn't even glance at us.

On the following Saturday my mother drove me to the Meet. She was looking anxious because Angela had gone off earlier on Mr Bodkin's new horse, and my mother had seen them going past the house sideways at an uncomfortable jog. At the Meet Angela was carried round in a dancing circle by the new horse.

'Brave girl, that,' said a fat man to my mother. 'Aren't you afraid she'll get run away with?'

'Oh, Angela's a good rider,' said my mother.

'I always put my children on quiet ponies,' said the fat man. 'Don't lose their nerve that way.' He moved off and my mother looked snubbed.

I looked round me. Quite a number of people were getting quiet horses out of horse-boxes. A lot of children wearing elegant velvet riding caps were sitting loosely and confidently on their ponies, all ready to move off. The grown-up people, wearing ratcatcher clothes, were chatting to each other. Andrew and James, wearing dirty jeans and rather torn jerseys, came up to us.

'Can Kate follow on foot with us and Blueprint?'

'Yes, of course,' said my mother. 'Where is your mother?'

'She's at home. Father thinks if the hounds come near the pigs she can fend them off better than he can.'

'Where are you going to draw first, Master?' a woman asked in a high confident voice.

'Longmans Wood. There are always cubs there and it's not too big.'

I moved aside with the Johnson boys and Blueprint.

'Nobody's talking to my mother,' I said.

'Just our friendly country manner,' said Andrew. 'Look, the Cardigans are talking to her.'

'They are strangers.'

'The others are all right, just a bit uncouth.' Andrew looked at the array of glossy Jaguars, Landrovers and Minis. 'Hunting people,' he added.

'Look at Angela,' said James.

The new horse was sweeping an apparently helpless Angela through the crowd, its ears back and head down. As she passed a very beautiful car she shied and kicked. There were exclamations of – 'Mind out!' – Need a hand?' – 'Steady on, whoa!' as the crowd scattered.

'Do my eyes deceive me?' Andrew looked up the road.

'They do not.' James's face was expressionless.

Down the road came Tom Foley driving his ancient Morris. Beside him sat Floss, looking unconcerned. Tom stopped and several voices called out – 'Hullo, Foley'.

Tom sat easily at the wheel, looking at the traditional scene.

'Morning, Foley,' shouted the Master.

Tom got out of his car. 'And how are you today?' he shouted at my mother, taking off Mr Johnson's hat to her. 'Hullo, Vicar.'

'Good morning,' said the vicar, rather surprised.

'Only Angela riding?' Tom Foley approached my mother, absolutely ignoring everyone else.

'Yes,' said my mother, looking up at him.

'I had a suit like that once,' said the vicar.

'Oh, this old thing.' Tom Foley looked down his long length. 'Like me to give the children a lift?' he asked my mother. 'Don't suppose you want to follow this lot.' His voice was louder, clearer, more confident than I had ever heard it – insolent.

'Not much,' said my mother honestly.

'Call your nosey hounds off my car,' said Tom genially to the Whip, pointing to where the hounds were milling round his ancient car and sniffing at Floss, who sat in the front seat snarling down at them.

'Sorry, sir. Here, Bashful, Dauntless, Terrible.' The Whip rode towards the Morris cracking his whip. The hounds moved away regretfully. If animals could smile I would have sworn that was just what the hounds were doing as they gathered obediently round the Whip. I sensed that what Floss had snarled at them was no ordinary snarl of a small bitch surrounded by large hounds. She looked smug.

'Weren't you in the same house as me?' A man in corduroy trousers and a tweed coat with leather patches at the elbows came up to Tom.

'Don't recollect it.' Tom spoke rudely and said to my mother: 'Angela's got quite a ride, I see.'

'We were in Wickhams,' said the man, but Tom was looking away.

'I daresay.' Tom sounded so off hand I blushed. 'Hounds moving off. Come on, you lot.' Tom took off the hat to my mother and led us to the Morris. We all climbed in. I held Blueprint in my arms. Tom started the engine and edged through the crowd. He drove rapidly round the corner of the road to the edge of the wood. 'They'll put the hounds in there,' Tom said to Floss. 'Bustle, old girl.' Floss nipped out of the car and raced to the edge of the wood.

'Now,' said Tom, and drove us furiously down the road to the great wood. 'You may be amused to watch the hunt,' he said to Andrew and James. 'I don't think you will find it unrewarding.' He went round to the back of the car and lifted the seat. Out streamed an incredible number of fox cubs.

'Now you behave and follow Blueprint. No skylarking.'
Blueprint raced up the hill through the bracken, followed by
a long line of fox cubs.

'Where are the old ones?' Andrew looked puzzled.

'They came ahead on foot.'

'I see.' Andrew and James left me alone with Tom Foley.
We walked without speaking to the badger sets, where we
found Blueprint sitting alone.

'Everything all right?'

'Yes,' said a fox voice.

Tom whistled and pigeons flew down from the trees.

'Just fly on patrol and keep me posted,' said Tom. 'And
now,' he said to me, 'we can watch ourselves.'

'But where are the foxes?'

'All around us. You won't see them.'

We walked quickly down to the road and sat down on a
bank to watch the hunt approach. First came the hounds,
trotting ahead of the huntsman and the Whip. They were
followed by Mr Bodkin on his nice quiet horse, a large
collection of children on admirable ponies, and all the
people who usually hunt, riding fine horses and looking at
each other rudely as hunting people do.

'Why do they all look so rude?' asked James.

'Nerves,' said Tom Foley, watching the cavalcade.

'Where is Floss?' I said.

'In the spinney now.' Tom grinned wolfishly. Blueprint
hurried up to us.

'What's up, Blueprint?'

'The cubs are there and some of their mothers, but most
of the grown foxes are not.'

'I told them to go ahead,' said Tom. 'They will be about
somewhere.' He didn't seem worried.

'When they've drawn the spinney where do they go next?'
I muttered.

'Across the Johnson land, I hope,' said Tom.

'Father will be livid. He's been up all night with
Gertrude.'

'The prize sow?' Tom looked amused.

'Yes. She farrowed.'

'Just look at Angela.' James admired Angela.

We watched Angela on the new mare bringing up the rear of the hunt. The mare was giving an excellent imitation of a rocking horse.

'She looks hot,' said James.

'Got a good grip on that animal's mane.' Tom grinned again. 'Listen.' We listened to the sound of the horn as the huntsman urged the hounds into the spinney. 'If we climb a bit higher we can get a better view.' Tom began loping up the hill and we followed. The huntsman blew his horn again. 'Now,' said Tom.

Almost immediately pandemonium broke loose in the spinney. Hounds bayed, people cantering alongside shouted, Angela went by far too fast, and a child we did not like much fell off his pony. The pony wheeled round and clattered off home with the loose stirrups swinging and his reins dangling. The child began to cry and a forceful woman jumped out of a Landrover to comfort him.

At the top of the hill Tom sat down and the boys and I sat beside him in a row with Blueprint.

'We can see home from here.' James pointed to the Johnsons' farm. 'There's mother leaning over the gate of the pig field.'

'That's our mother with her,' I said.

Below us in the spinney the hounds were giving tongue. A pigeon dropped at Tom's feet and said: 'Floss is in position.'

'Any minute now then.' Tom was smiling.

The hounds broke into full cry. They seemed to sweep round the spinney in a circle and then stream out of it across the fields towards the Johnsons'. Tom stood up and let out a blood curdling yell of 'Gone awaaay!' pointing towards the Johnsons' farm with his long arm. Below us the field gathered up their reins and clattered down the road. The Master was cantering ahead. We could see from where we sat that the hounds, although they had their noses to the ground, were chasing nothing. Floss ran a little way with them, then ran across the road and up the hill towards us. She arrived panting and wagging her bushy tail.

'Where did you send them Floss?' James looked respectfully at the little dog.

'They are calling on Gertrude first,' she said.

'Overdoing it a bit, aren't you, old girl?' Tom stroked Floss.

'Couldn't resist,' Floss panted.

We watched the hounds in full cry across the Johnsons' land.

'Father will be furious.' Andrew was standing up, hopping from one foot to another. We could see Mrs Johnson and our mother brace themselves by the gate of the pig field and Mr Johnson coming out of the farmyard with Joker.

'That ain't no cub, they must be on to a fox,' the huntsman was shouting to the Master.

'Then stop them.' The Master was having trouble holding his horse, and we saw Angela streak past him on the new mare, shouting: 'So sorry, so sorry, she's running away with me.'

In the corn stubble we heard derisory jeers, and when I looked round I saw eight or nine dog foxes crouching behind us. The whole field galloped past.

'Make them sweat. So bad for them when they aren't fit.' Blueprint is essentially kind and fair.

'Watch now.' Tom peered from under the brim of his hat. The hounds seemed to drown Mrs Johnson and our mother in a wave of white and tan and then charged up towards Gertrude's hut.

'Ah,' said Tom.

Furious and ponderous, Gertrude barred the entrance. The hounds milled round her. We could not hear Gertrude, but as suddenly as they had surrounded her the hounds reformed and streamed away.

Mr Johnson was yelling what I believe is known as 'a stream of epithets' at the Master and huntsman. Our mothers held fast to the gate and Joker ran behind the hounds, snapping.

'Father *is* in good form,' said Andrew.

'Yes.' James's eyes were shining. 'Ooh! Look at Angela!'

Angela was circling round the field. The new mare had her head down and was bucking with a twisting motion which brought her each time nearer to where the Master was apologising to Mr Johnson. As she finished her circle she kicked the Master's horse, making it rear up and nearly unseat the Master. The hounds were out of sight. We watched the field disappear after them and our mother and the Johnsons go into the farmhouse.

'Better not disturb her any more,' we heard the boys' father say, his voice hoarse with anger. Angela was lost to sight.

'Can't see anyone buying that animal in a hurry.' Tom got up slowly. We followed him into the wood, led by Floss. Apart from the jays and magpies making remarks on the edge of the wood, all was silence compared with the haunting voices of the hounds fading away down the valley.

Floss and Tom stopped at the badgers' sets. 'Everybody all right?' Tom enquired in a conversational voice.

A vixen came from behind a tree and fawned like a dog, grinning silently, her little sharp teeth bared, her ears laid back and her brush trailing low, and a whole multitude of cubs appeared from the bracken and out of the badger sets. A badger followed the last batch, remarking amiably: 'You smell.'

'Where are all the dog foxes?' I watched the cubs begin a game, flitting in and out among the trees, watched by bright-eyed vixens.

'Some were in the corn stubble.'

'We are here now.' A dignified fox trotted out from the trees.

'Enjoy yourselves?' enquired Floss.

'Very much.' The fox leered.

'Floss,' I said, 'what were you up to in that spinney?'

'Just warming them up.' Floss licked her chest and then, after scratching one ear hard, lay down.

'Next time they can manage alone, I daresay,' said Blueprint.

'I wonder where the other dog foxes are. There should be at least four more.' Blueprint looked at each in turn and tucked his tail out of the way of a cub who was creeping up on him to tweak it.

'Ah, here you all are.' Joker appeared suddenly in the clearing, followed by four dog foxes.

'Where were you all?' Blueprint asked.

One of the dog foxes began yelping with laughter and then rolled playfully on his back. 'With Gertrude,' he said.

'Gertrude farrowed last night.' Andrew sounded anxious. 'You didn't eat – ?'

'Oh, no, no,' said another fox. 'We got delayed so we popped in with Gertrude for a bit.'

'I wonder what my father would say.' Andrew looked suspiciously at the foxes.

'He won't know, will he?'

'I thought you smelt rather nasty,' a vixen snapped at one of Gertrude's visitors jealously.

'One wonders what has become of Angela,' murmured Tom.

'Yes.' James looked anxious. 'Can't you call a pigeon, Tom?'

From under his hat Tom whistled and a pigeon cooed above our heads.

'Won't come down because of the foxes.' Tom smiled.

'Quite safe for you all to go home.' A badger showed its striped nose from a hole. 'We like a bit of peace and quiet.'

Floss nestled against Tom. We stood up, feeling unwanted.

'You will all know your way another time,' said the badger courteously. 'Very welcome, of course.'

'The hounds know what to do in future.' Floss spoke complacently. 'Very handsome they are.'

We watched as the foxes gathered their families and moved off.

'Hounds get lost in this wood, it's so big.' Andrew looked down at Tom. 'Come on,' he said, and we followed Blueprint and Joker down the hill.

'Back to work.' Joker looked over his shoulder at

Blueprint, who looked embarrassed. 'I bet those hounds have fun.' Joker broke into a gallop in answer to a distant whistle.

'I should think everyone has had fun,' said James.

We accompanied the boys to their house and went into the kitchen, where our mother was helping Mrs Johnson.

'Hullo,' said my mother. 'Anyone seen Angela?'

'Don't worry,' said Mrs Johnson.

Mr Johnson came in and took off his gumboots. 'Gertrude *seems* all right,' he said.

'I'm sure she is.' My mother spoke soothingly.

'Nothing sure about it. That's a remarkable sow. She barred the entrance of her hut. Noble creature.'

'She's pretty savage,' said Mrs Johnson.

'So would you be savage if you had just had fourteen children, and a yelling pack of hounds tried to burst into the maternity ward.'

'It's an idea,' said my mother.

'I shall ring up the Master when he gets home,' Mr Johnson mused.

'Do,' said my mother. 'My husband has got to too. He's got to warn the hunt off the Broughton shoot.'

'Ha, ha!' said Joker from under the table.

'The Master's going to have a happy evening,' said Mrs Johnson.

'Well, Gertrude is a valuable animal.'

'From what I know of Gertrude she is quite able to look after herself,' said Mrs Johnson placidly.

I left the Johnsons' with my mother and we rejoined Blueprint, who had been tactfully waiting by the gate.

'Those poor men are still fishing,' said my mother as we walked up the river.

'Any luck?' my mother enquired kindly.

'No, none.' The fatter Mr Cardigan looked up as we paused above him. 'Plenty of fish about. One can see them all the time. But it's enjoyable even if you catch nothing.' The fat Mr Cardigan climbed up the bank and stood beside us looking down at the sun-flecked water. 'We've both seen so many birds and I thought I saw a pair of foxes and an otter.'

'Surely not with the hunt raging down the valley. Come and have tea, Mr Cardigan.' From my mother's voice I knew she felt guilty that the Cardigans had caught no fish.

'Thank you. We should love to and then perhaps we shall have better luck with the evening rise.'

'Perhaps,' said Blueprint.

As we reached home we heard the clatter of horses coming down the road and saw the Master and Angela riding slowly towards us.

'Had a good day?' asked my mother, who was not in the least interested.

'Remarkable, remarkable,' said the Master. 'Hounds ran right down the valley. Must have got on the scent of a fox.' He pulled up his horse and let the reins lie loose on its neck.

'Come and have tea,' said my mother affably. I could see she was relieved to see Angela all in one piece.

'I'll take your horse,' I said.

The Master got off, handed me the reins, and I led the horse round to the stable yard.

'Want a drink?' I asked.

'No, eat,' said the horse. 'I drank at the ford.'

I got the horse some hay and put it in a loose box.

'Had one hell of a day,' said the horse as I loosened its girths. 'I could do with a beer.'

I went into the house and opened a bottle of beer and took it to the horse in a bucket.

'Put up quite a show, didn't we?' The horse souped up the beer. 'No need for that mare to kick me though.'

'She overacts,' I said. I went indoors, where I could hear voises raised.

'What's up?' I said to my mother, who was making tea.

'The Cardigans have told him hunting is ridiculous,' said my mother with a faint smile. 'Take this tray.' I carried in the tray.

'Forms the character,' the Master was saying.

'Not like fishing, you need patience for that,' the thin Mr Cardigan said, rather nastily I thought.

My mother came in carrying another tray.

'Very rude, that Johnson chap.' The Master stood in front of the fireplace with his legs apart.

'Pigs,' I said.

'Ah, yes.'

'He's going to complain to you,' I said and left the room.

Upstairs Blueprint and I sat on the window-ledge beside Mr Bull's cage. 'Everybody will know exactly what to do next time,' Mr Bull piped cheerfully.

The mouse came out of its hole. 'Nobody got killed.'

'I nearly did.' Angela came into the room. 'Old Bodkin is furious. He says the whole neighbourhood knows what that "new thing", as he calls her, is like now.'

Vice uncurled and stretched on my bed. He scratched the bedhead violently.

'I'm aching from head to foot.' Angela started to undress. 'But it was worth it.'

'You and Gertrude seem to be the heroines of the day,' said the mouse.

'Don't forget Floss,' said Blueprint.

'Oh, Floss.' Vice began licking himself all over. 'Floss is wily.'

'More wily than me?' Blueprint leant heavily against me.

'Much more,' said Vice between long scraping licks. 'All the animals except Floss and me and Mr Bull here had to be told what to do.'

'What did you do?' asked Blueprint innocently.

'I directed operations.' Vice stared offensively at Blueprint.

'Did you now?' said the mouse, and before Vice could pounce vanished down its hole.

'Is Angela all right?' Our mother came into the room.

'Yes, just going to have a bath.' I saw my mother was frowning in a worried way.

'How is the tea party?' Angela started off towards the bathroom.

'Awful,' said my mother. 'Snapping each other's heads off like pekinese. You would think to hear them talk that they were hunting each other, not foxes and fish.'

⟫ 12 ⟪

Angela lay in the bath covered with soap, and Blueprint leant over the edge licking whatever bits of her he could reach.

'We should go and help mother,' I said.

'Why?'

'She's stuck between hunting and fishing.' Blueprint licked Angela's arm.

'All right.' Angela got out of the bath and dressed, combing her hair demurely behind her ears.

We went downstairs where Vice was sitting in the afternoon sun by the open front door. He was watching the birds whirling and circling in swoops which ended each time by my bedroom window. We paused a moment before joining the tea party to listen to the birds and Mr Bull's piping.

'They are having a good laugh.' Vice joined us and we went into the sitting-room where there was an awkward grown-up silence reigning.

'Had a good day?' The Cardigans greeted Angela.

'Yes, thank you.' Angela shot an angelic smile at the Master. Vice stalked across the room to where the two Mr Cardigans sat and began weaving in and out of their legs in an intricate pattern, bending his body sideways to press it against their shins and purring.

'Fond of cats?' I asked.

'Well, as a matter of fact they make us both sneeze, so we don't know much about them.'

'He means he hates cats,' said Blueprint, wagging his tail in a hospitable sort of way at the Master of Hounds, who instantly gave him a biscuit.

'Shall I remove him?' said my mother.

'Oh no, please. We both take antihistamine so it doesn't matter,' said the elder Mr Cardigan. 'One can't deny oneself all the joys of life just because they make you sneeze.'

'Do you hear that, Vice? You are one of the joys of life.' My mother laughed.

'Horses and dogs make us sneeze too.' The thin Mr Cardigan passed his cup politely to my mother.

'No need for you to go near horses if you are against hunting.' The Master used rather a hearty voice to be rude. 'Now, Angela is a born rider. You should have seen her on that wild creature of Bodkin's today.'

'I did,' said my mother.

'Natural hands and a beautiful seat,' said the Master.

Vice suddenly sprang at our father's favourite chair and scraped it viciously, lashing his tail and looking at my mother to see if she would try to stop him. Our mother went on pouring tea.

'Needs real courage to ride a thing like that.' The Master spoke with his mouth full of biscuit and a small shower of crumbs seemed to blow out with every word. 'Of course, he'll never sell it.'

'Well,' said Angela, with her mouth full, 'I'm going to hunt her this season.'

'Angela has volunteered to teach the younger children to ride.' The Master addressed himself to my mother.

'Oh,' she said.

'Is she mad?' I muttered to Blueprint, leaning down to give him a piece of cake.

'Crafty,' said Vice, passing me as he went to the window. 'Like Floss,' he added.

'I shall have to ask my husband,' said our mother. 'Oh, here he comes. I know he wants to see you, Master.' Our mother watched our father drive slowly past the window towards the garage. Blueprint began to shriek and yell and thump his tail as though he had not seen our father for a month.

'Time we went.' One of the Cardigans sneezed and the other stood up. They thanked my mother politely and gave a cold nod to the Master.

'Just the sort of people to have allergies. Too frightened to hunt and can't catch any fish.' The Master watched them go. 'Townees,' he added.

'I was brought up in London,' our mother said tartly. 'They know a lot about birds and fish.'

'Bet they don't shoot,' said the Master. 'Hullo, George,' he said as our father came in with Blueprint.

'Good afternoon,' said our father.

'What's this you want to see me about, George?' Hardly anyone calls my father George. He simply hates it.

'Shooting,' said my father, 'and hunting.'

'Shooting?'

'Yes. The Broughton Syndicate want you to keep off their land.' My father sounded rather pleased to impart the news. 'Your hounds disturb their pheasants and partridges. I act for them.'

'But that's ridiculous.'

'Quite legal.' Our father accepted a cup of tea from our mother and smiled.

'Legal be damned. It limits the field of the hunt quite dreadfully.'

'Why don't you try the Great Wood?' my mother asked soothingly.

'I can't. I always lose the whole pack in there.'

'Well, there it is,' said our father. 'It's trespassing and that Syndicate are a tough lot.' Our father flushed a little and our mother looked anxious, as when he got excited his ulcers hurt.

'A lot of company directors who shoot foxes!' exclaimed the Master.

'I thought you were a company director yourself,' I said.

'Help me clear away tea,' said my mother. Vice jumped on to our father's lap and Blueprint leant against his leg with his big head on his knee, gazing into his face.

'There is such a thing as tact,' said my mother to me in the hall.

'Listen,' said Angela. We stood in the hall, our hands holding trays of dirty cups and saucers.

'They come down at weekends and blaze off their guns.

They shoot foxes and I wouldn't be surprised if their keepers trapped them too. They are a bunch of Londoners who just come and throw their money about. They are just like that couple of old maids you and Johnson have let your fishing to, they – '

'I believe, er, Johnson would be happier if you kept off his farm,' our father said gently. 'I act for him too.'

'Happier!' Angela bumped open the kitchen door with her behind and we washed up without speaking, but each of us knew the others were thinking of the exchange of words Mr Johnson had had that morning with the Master.

'Why do we all call him Master?' I said. 'It's silly.'

'I must see he drinks milk tonight,' said my mother, which meant that she knew and we knew our father hated being called George and also hated rows so that his ulcers came to life.

'And I,' cried Angela suddenly, 'am going to every Pony Club meeting, every gymkhana. I am going to hunt twice a week.'

'Then you will be fully occupied,' our mother said drily. I went upstairs to see Mr Bull and refresh him with the news of the tea party.

'Can you get me some cheese?' said the mouse.

I went down to the larder and snipped a bit of Cheddar from a hunk of cheese. I gave it to the mouse, who hurried into its hole with it, and then I ran across the garden to join Angela.

'What's this about the Pony Club?' I asked.

'I can train them perfectly if I have them. That mare and I can meet all the horses and ponies from miles around.'

'What about it?'

'We can teach them too.'

'Oh,' I said, the light dawning. We walked on to the field Mr Bodkin kept his horses in. The new mare was rolling on her back, rolling and rolling and trying to get upright on the upward slope of the field.

'It's a perpetual challenge,' said the old horse, accepting a carrot. 'Enjoyed myself today,' he added, munching. 'Thought you two overdid it a bit.'

'Had to establish a reputation.' The new mare joined us. 'Nobody will dare buy me now,' she added smugly.

'I'm stiff all over,' said Angela.

'Come off it,' said the old horse. Angela laughed.

'We are going to hunt, go to all the gymkhanas and Pony Club meetings,' she said. The new mare whinnied. 'Someone may try and ride you, one of the judges or something.'

'I shall lie down and roll on him.' The new mare backed away and began to eat grass.

We walked home to find our mother leaning on the bridge parapet and looking downstream.

'How is father?' I said.

'Gone mad I think,' said our mother.

'Mad?'

'Yes, he let the Cardigans pay him for the fishing in cash and has now given it to the Master of Hounds for the R.S.P.C.A.'

'He's a great supporter,' I said.

'What about our education?' said Angela.

'Ah,' said our mother. 'Look, there's a woodpecker.'

'I saw a bullfinch today,' I said to test her.

'There aren't any bullfinches round here,' she said sadly. 'Only your poor creature in its cage.'

'He's perfectly happy,' I said.

'I don't like caged birds. Just look at all those fish, and those poor men catch nothing. It's funny.'

'Very funny,' said Angela.

After supper I went into the wood. The river makes quite a different noise at night if you listen carefully. An otter ambled along the bank and I said 'good evening'. The otter stopped. In the half-light I could see its whiskery face.

'You gave us a good laugh today,' said the otter. 'I like you.'

'Do you get on with foxes?' I asked.

'We don't speak unless necessary.'

'Do you speak to the other otters now?'

'Not necessary.'

'Why not necessary?'

'That Floss and your Blueprint and Joker told the hounds what to do.'

'Will they remember?'

'Oh, yes, they are pleased.'

'Why?'

'Well, if they *really* hunt us we bite them. Now they are just going to have jolly bathing parties along the rivers. Everyone will be pleased. Do you like slugs?'

'No,' I said.

'We eat a lot of slugs and mice and beetles.'

'What about fish?'

'Only on occasion.' The otter drifted into the shadows and I got up and walked on and out of the wood into the Johnsons' pig field. I went to Gertrude's hut. Gertrude's tiny eye glistened in the dark. I could just make out the shapes of her fourteen piglets lying against her flank.

'I wanted to thank you for what you did this morning,' I said.

Gertrude grunted.

'You were very brave.'

'Pigs are brave.' Gertrude's eye rolled a little.

'What is the meaning of life, Gertrude?' I asked.

'To produce bacon.'

'There must be something beyond bacon,' I said.

'Eggs.' Gertrude's bulk heaved at her own joke and all the disturbed piglets shifted and made tiny complaining grunts. 'No good being metaphysical on a farm,' said Gertrude.

'Do cows think the same as you?'

'More or less.'

'Bacon,' I said, feeling a tear roll down my cheek.

'Don't be a fool. Bacon, milk, eggs – we all live happy lives.' Gertrude grunted.

'Sheep,' I said.

'Wool and mutton,' said Gertrude. 'It's life.' She shut her tiny eye and I felt dismissed. I went to look for Andrew and told him about Gertrude.

'Ah,' said Andrew. 'Meaning of life my foot.'

'Will you come and see the badgers tomorrow?' I asked.

'Yes. I want to see Tom.'

But next morning when we had climbed up through the wood to the badgers' sets, Tom was not there.

'I wonder where he is.' Andrew looked round him and then went across to the bushes and peered under. 'Everything's gone.'

'Was the car in the quarry?'

'No, it wasn't, now I come to think of it.'

We stood uncertainly on the edge of the hollow.

'Pigeons?' I asked.

'There don't seem to be any.'

We listened to the silence and the faint noise of the wind in the trees. Andrew knelt down and spoke politely down a large badger set. 'Did Tom leave a message by any chance?'

'No message,' a grumbling voice answered.

'Oh, heavens!' I said. 'Here's a trapped fox.'

'Where?' Andrew joined me.

A young fox was lying on its side staring up at us. So fiercely had it fought when trapped that the chain to which the trap was attached was madly twisted.

'Keep still,' I said to the fox. The fox watched us.

'It's all right,' said Andrew, 'but you have twisted the beastly thing so much I can't step on the release.' Andrew strained with his strong hands to open the trap. The fox looked at him beadily.

'They usually knock us on the head with the butt of their guns,' it said.

'Keep still,' said Andrew, sweating. He forced the trap open slowly and the fox snatched its paw out.

'Where do you come from?' said Andrew.

'Not far.'

'We will carry you.'

'You smell,' said the fox.

'You must put up with it.' Andrew picked the fox up gently and waited while I went along the edge of the wood and let all the little birds out of the bird traps.

'Crazy,' said the fox.

'Anyone know where this cub comes from?' Andrew asked down one of the badgers' sets.

'Its mother is somewhere about,' came a sleepy answer.

The cub yelped and we waited. Presently the cub pricked its ears. 'There's my mum,' it said, and we saw a vixen watching us from the other side of the clearing. Andrew put the cub down and it limped away to its mother.

'Stupid fool, I told you not to go there,' she said.

'Doesn't seem to be much sympathy about.' Andrew dusted fox hairs off the front of his shirt. 'I wonder where he's gone.' He looked round the empty clearing. 'Does he live here all the year round?' Andrew asked down a hole.

'Depends on the weather,' came a sleepy answer.

'Just when we're getting organized,' Andrew grumbled.

'I know he comes and goes,' I said.

'Goes where?'

'I don't know.' Tom's disappearance gave me a sense of defeat.

'Don't be downhearted.' Andrew looked at me quite kindly. 'He'll come back.'

'When?'

'When will Tom come back?' Andrew asked down a set.

'Can't you leave us in peace,' a cross voice answered.

'The Cardigans paid my father for the fishing in cash,' I said, 'and he gave it to the R.S.P.C.A. He handed it straight to the Master.'

Andrew laughed. 'I posted them their stolen money,' he said.

'I must tell Gertrude,' I said. 'She seems to have a funny sense of humour. What is metaphysical?'

'I've no idea.' Andrew led the way downhill through the wood. 'Nothing to do with us.'

13

We met Angela riding the new mare. The moment she saw us the mare reared up, shied and put her head down.

'Don't be silly,' said Angela. 'I nearly fell off.'

'Sorry,' said the mare, but she didn't look it.

'What's her name?' asked Andrew.

'Mr Bodkin calls her "that thing".'

'She should have a name,' I said.

'I shall call her Margot Fonteyn,' said Angela.

'Why?' said the mare, turning her neck to nibble at Angela's foot in the stirrup. 'Who's she?'

'She's a dancer,' said Angela.

'Not as good as me, I bet,' said the mare. 'I'm sure she can't do this.' The mare gave a sideways leap and reared up on end. Angela fell off.

'You fool,' said Angela, getting up.

'Sorry,' said the mare, looking amused. 'Call me Marge.'

'All right, Marge.' Angela climbed back on to Marge.

'Marge! What an awful name.' Andrew watched Angela ride off through the wood. 'It's funny about Tom. I shall ask Joker. He's rather thick with Floss.'

We met Joker walking in a docile way behind Mr Johnson.

'Seen Floss?' enquired Andrew.

'Gone away. I'm busy now.' Joker glanced at Mr Johnson.

'If either of you see Tom Foley will you ask him to come and give me a hand tomorrow?'

'We haven't seen him,' we said.

'Then I shall have to manage on my own.' Mr Johnson walked on.

'I believe Joker knows,' said Andrew. 'And the badgers must too, but for some reason they won't tell.'

'Let's ask Gertrude.'

'Gertrude is busy. There's James. Let's ask him.'

But James did not know, and all the animals we met gave rude or evasive answers.

The weeks passed and we all went to the various gymkhanas to watch Angela and Marge perform. In the ring Marge would jump like a dream, play musical chairs and win races. But she was not popular with the judges who got nipped or kicked when they came up to pat her, nor with the admiring children who unwisely asked for rides. We all moved about among the children's ponies and Blueprint and Marge talked to them. When the hounds were brought to the Shows, Blueprint mixed freely with them.

'It is like canvassing for an election,' Blueprint explained. 'I brainwash them into thinking they do not like chasing foxes.'

'Any success?' I asked.

'Well, yes.' Blueprint enjoyed his encounters with hounds. 'The bitches think it's a good thing for their puppies to pretend, but the dogs want their puppies to be manly. They are on the Conservative side except for a few who would vote Labour or Liberal if they had the misfortune to be born human.'

'Misfortune?'

'Well, yes, having to work for their living like you all do. Just look at your father. Ulcers. *We* don't get ulcers.'

'I hadn't thought of it in that light,' I said.

'They all laugh though.' Blueprint looked pleased with his social success.

Angela and Marge went cubbing on Tuesdays and Saturdays and the rest of us watched the foxes, young and old, who gathered in the sanctuary of the Great Wood. Since foxes are highly intelligent, it soon became unnecessary to go ourselves. We just told the local foxes in our wood.

Our father was rung up one night by the Master, who accused his Broughton-shoot clients of shooting and trapping foxes. My father answered rather huffily and told the Master that if he made such unproven accusations he was heading for litigation.

'What is litigation?' I asked my mother.

'Litigation pays for your education,' she said ambiguously.

'Ah,' I said, none the wiser.

'The fact remains we haven't killed a single cub this season.' The Master had the sort of voice one could hear down the telephone from the next room, and our father held the receiver a yard from his ear.

'I hear that you are having very good days though,' said my father.

'Never see a fox. Can't get the hounds blooded.'

'Too bad,' said my father unsympathetically.

'Your daughter will tell you.'

'She seems to enjoy herself very much,' said my father, protecting his ear with one hand.

'Your daughter should join a circus.'

'That's an idea. Goodbye.' Our father laid the receiver back on its cradle.

'First of September on Saturday,' I said to Angela in my room.

'I'm hunting,' said Angela.

'Partridge shooting begins, you idiot,' I said.

'So it does.' Mr Bull looked at us wisely. 'You can't hide the partridges and foxes in the same place. It would be asking too much.'

'It would,' said Vice.

'The foxes will go as usual to the same place,' Blueprint remarked. 'You can't muddle them now.'

'And pheasant shooting begins in a month,' I moaned.

'If only Floss were here and Tom.'

'I will arrange it.' Vice looked incredibly sly. 'I know one of the keepers' cats.' He left the room and we looked at each other.

'We can't leave it to the cats.' Blueprint looked worried.

'You must,' piped Mr Bull.

'Blueprint, do you think Vice and the keepers' cat are the proper people to hide the partridges?'

'I will talk to Joker.'

'The shooting people all stay at the hotel for their weekends.'

'Good business,' said Blueprint.

'What on earth do you know about it?'

'I may not be able to read, but I can hear.' Blueprint went away looking very dignified. I went down to see James who, when I reminded him about the beginning of the shooting season, said: 'Oh, my, my!'

'I wish Tom would come back,' I said. 'He's been away weeks.'

We walked moodily to the pig field, which was now filled with immense sows surrounded by their rooting, romping families. Gertrude's were especially gay, cantering about in their jerky way like small people in bikinis. Gertrude watched them with her crafty eyes shining out of her great jowly face.

'Hullo, Gertrude,' said James.

Gertrude grunted.

'Father is going to keep all Gertrude's.' James looked at Gertrude with pride.

'He is keeping them for breeding.' Andrew picked up the thick stick his father kept near the gate for the special purpose of scratching his pigs and scraped it along Gertrude's side.

'Not bacon then,' I said, and looked at Gertrude with relief.

'Not this time,' said Gertrude.

' "Parting is such sweet sorrow" doesn't apply to farmers,' I said. 'They never see their dear ones again.'

'Sad,' said James. 'One shouldn't think of it.'

'Even if this lot are not to become bacon, their children will,' I said.

'Don't be so morbid, Kate.' Gertrude swayed her enormous flank closer to the stick. 'Even you will be buried one day,' she added maliciously.

Joker barked from the next field. He was rounding up a flock of sheep with Mr Johnson watching.

'I wish Tom would come back and give me a hand.' Mr Johnson watched Joker doing all the work as he stood leaning on his stick. 'They like Tom.' One of the ewes turned and glared at Joker and stamped her foot.

'Good wool,' remarked Mr Johnson. 'Should get good wool next year.'

'I don't mind the wool,' I said. 'It's the mutton.'

'You eat it,' said Mr Johnson without looking at me.

'Do you?'

'Not my own. How could you eat a bit of an animal you

had raised from birth, put a lot of love and work into, spent money you can't afford on, gone without holidays for, loved.' Mr Johnson's face was expressionless.

'Why are you a farmer then?' James looked at his father in surprise.

Mr Johnson laughed. 'I love animals,' he said. 'Look at that ewe annoying Joker. I give my animals very happy lives. Look at those pigs. Never do a stroke of work. Everything is provided for them. They don't have to sit in offices, do they?'

'No,' I said, visualizing Gertrude running an office.

'They don't get crushed in tubes and buses in noisy towns.'

'I can see Gertrude crushing a lot of people herself.' James began to laugh.

'Gertrude has brains,' said Mr Johnson, and walked up to close the gate Joker had driven the sheep though.

We went round a corner out of sight with Joker and told him about the cats and the first of September.

'I'm no wiser than you are,' said Joker. 'If Floss were here she would know what to do.'

'Floss isn't.'

'Then ask your bullfinch.' Joker lapped water from the trough and went into the farmhouse after his master.

'None of the animals are very helpful.' James looked disconsolate.

'I am.' Blueprint, who had been following at our heels all this time, suddenly left us and we saw him cutting across country to the Broughton land.

'He is friends with the keepers' dogs,' said James.

In my room Mr Bull was eating seed and the mouse was waiting for the odd seed to come his way.

'Vice and the keepers' cats are in cahoots,' I said.

'Don't care for cats.' The mouse nibbled a seed.

'Blueprint has gone to join them.'

'Why?' asked the mouse.

'He's made friends with the keepers' dogs, of course.' Mr Bull drank a sip of water, fluffed out his feathers, and jumped up on to his top perch.

'Angela has gone off to arrange a specially good hunt with Marge.'

The mouse tittered.

'It still leaves us with the terrible problem of where to put the partridges,' said James, stroking the mouse with one careful finger.

'Do you children feel left out?' Mr Bull had a nasty way of arriving at conclusions.

'Yes,' said James honestly.

'Then leave it to Vice. He knows what he is doing.'

Neither Mr Bull or the mouse would tell us any more, and in the woods and fields the few animals we met just laughed.

On the first of September we were worried stiff. Angela had gone off rather early, riding Marge. Vice had disappeared. James and I and Blueprint climbed the hill from the top of which we had a good view of the keepers' cottages and the Broughton shoot.

We had taken Blueprint to the hotel the evening before. The Syndicate arrived in their Jaguars, and Blueprint had had a word with a pair of smart labradors. We had seen the hotel-keeper help his guests carry in their guns. Blueprint had returned from his conversation with the labradors looking complacent, but had told us nothing, so as we three lay at the top of the hill both James and I felt rather cross with Blueprint.

It was not long before the keepers came and let their dogs out of their kennels. Both keepers carried guns and waited, chatting to each other.

'I wish I knew what Vice is up to.' James fidgeted.

'It's his joke,' said Blueprint, lying with his nose on his paws looking down at the keepers.

'I wish you would tell us.' James stroked Blueprint, who only rolled his eyes and wagged his tail faintly.

Presently we saw the Syndicate arrive, talk to the keepers and discuss how they would walk in line.

'They are starting,' I said.

The guns formed themselves into a line and began walking slowly across the nearest field of stubble. Blueprint cocked his ears as though he could hear them.

'It will be a massacre,' I said.

'Wait and watch,' Blueprint growled.

The guns walked across the first field and four pheasants flew up explosively.

'No danger for them for another month.' Andrew had joined us, crawling through the undergrowth at the edge of the wood. A stoat passed us and snickered.

'No need to laugh. The game larder has been empty for weeks,' said Blueprint. 'And small thanks to you.'

'Watch,' said Andrew.

The line of guns left the stubble and crossed a farm track into a field of kale. They carried their guns cocked.

'Look silly, don't they?' James was watching carefully.

We lay where we were for an hour, watching the sportsmen walk on in a line.

'Funny,' said Andrew.

'Very funny.' Blueprint was now standing up, panting.

'The partridges seem to have gone.' James looked very puzzled.

The guns wheeled in a wide circle and still no partridges rose in front of them. We saw the gamekeepers' cat sitting watching on one side of the cottage doorsteps.

'Funny,' said James, echoing Andrew.

'Funnier in a moment. Listen.' Blueprint and the cat below us both had cocked ears. Far away behind the big hill between us and home we heard hounds in full cry.

'Hounds,' I said.

We listened intently with our eyes still fixed on the Syndicate who were, one would imagine, getting hot and tired. The sound of the hunt swelled round the far side of the wood and we could see, though we could not hear, the Syndicate making angry signals to the keepers. Still no partridge rose in fearful covey, still the Syndicate walked on with guns cocked. Presently they stopped to confer. The hounds came nearer, and with joy we watched them running in a wedge about two miles away.

'There go Angela and Marge.' James had very sharp eyes.

The pack swept along the very edge of the Syndicate's lane. Sounds of angry protest came up to us from the sportsmen and we saw them get into their cars and drive off.

'Not a single partridge,' said James.

'Any point in waiting and watching now?' I could hear from his voice that James was hungry.

'None at all.' Blueprint rolled in the long grass, scratching his spine against a stick.

'I do think you are mean,' I said to him. 'You might tell us where the partridges are.'

'You will enjoy hearing the shooting people ringing up your father about the hunting people.'

'Gorgeous,' said James. 'You are lucky.'

We walked up through the woods, meeting small parties of foxes as we went, returning to their homes. They stood aside politely as we passed and we greeted them. Before we got to the Johnsons' farm we met Angela hacking slowly home on Marge.

'Enjoy yourself, Marge?' I asked.

'Yes. I'm going to have a red ribbon for my tail.' Marge nuzzled me nicely.

'Blueprint knows where the partridges are and won't tell us,' I said to Angela.

Angela looked furiously at Blueprint. 'How could you!' she said.

'You'd be frightened if I told you,' said Blueprint.

'Nonsense,' said Angela. Blueprint's tail dropped.

'Vice isn't frightened, nor was the keepers' cat,' I said.

'Vice knew you would be frightened,' Blueprint's tail was down.

'Is he bringing them back?' Andrew was practical.

'Oh yes.'

'And he isn't afraid?'

'It's his sort of place.' Blueprint sounded rather miserable.

'His sort of place?' Angela went white. 'Oh, NO!'

'Yes,' Blueprint whined.

'The haunted house,' whispered James.

❧ 14 ❧

Once long ago when we were small we had all four set out to visit the haunted house, but for perfectly good reasons which we all thought up, we had turned back.

'This time we must go,' said Angela. 'If Vice can, we can. We are older now anyway. Let's meet by the Johnsons' bridge after supper.' Angela trotted off on Marge.

After supper, which had been interrupted by Sir Somebody Something of the Broughton Syndicate ringing up my father and asking him to complain to the hunt, Angela and I with Blueprint went down through the wood carrying torches. We met the boys and Joker waiting for us.

'Anyone complain about the shoot yet?' James enquired.

'They certainly did, but father said if the hunt hadn't actually set hoof on their land he could do nothing.'

'There were no birds to disturb either,' said James.

'Come on,' said Andrew, and I could tell he was nervous. That house is not a place anyone goes to. All anyone knows is that it's a very old house in the Great Wood in a clearing and that it belongs to nobody. As I walked behind Andrew and Angela, with James and the dogs behind me, I tried to remember whether I knew anyone who had ever seen it and I couldn't.

'Does anyone know the way?' Andrew asked after we had been walking along the edge of the wood for some time.

'No,' we all said. 'It's secret.'

'I once heard my father say it is beyond the bend in the river,' James volunteered.

'Then it must be right back inside the wood.'

'Yes,' said James.

'Quite hidden.'

'Yes,' said James.

'Vice is the limit,' said Andrew presently.

'You tell him.' Angela was cross.

The river swept in a huge arc and then quite suddenly became wide, silent and dark under the trees, gliding oilily close to the woods. A water rat plopped into the river and we all jumped and stood still. It was dusk and in the wood the owls were beginning to hoot. Andrew shone his torch about him. 'There's no path into the wood.'

'Here's a tiny one,' said Angela after a time. 'It looks used.'

Andrew started walking up it slowly. We followed.

'Oh!' Andrew stopped suddenly. We stood in a row on the edge of a clearing and stared. On the edge of it crouched a low stone house. There was glass in the windows and the glass blinked back a reflection from the stars. There was absolute silence. Andrew and Angela shone the beams of their torches across the clearing towards the house. We stood hesitating. Suddenly there was a loud moaning yell ending in a shriek. We turned as one and ran. Andrew, running the fastest, tripped, Angela fell over him and James and I on top of them.

'Having trouble?' said Vice.

'You fiend,' said Andrew, shining his torch at Vice's green eyes. We all got up, ashamed and silent.

'This way.' Vice tripped lightly with his tail in the air across the clearing and round the corner of the house.

Shining their torches, Andrew and Angela picked out quantities of partridges crouched in the grass.

'I see,' said Angela. 'You wicked thing!' And she began to laugh. We all joined in and the dogs wagged their tails.

'I'll take them back later,' said Vice. 'And from October onwards the pheasants can roost in the trees.'

'Very jolly,' I said. 'And what's in the house?'

'The door is locked.' Vice sounded a bit annoyed.

'Then I'll unlock it.' Tom Foley spoke from behind us. 'Bit nosey, aren't you?' He spoke amiably. 'You the banshee?' He bent down to stroke Vice. The dogs wagged their tails.

'Where have you been, Tom?' Andrew wanted to speak quickly before any reference could be made to our recent panic.

'Scotland.'

'Why?'

'The Glorious Twelfth.' Tom was grinning.

'Grouse,' said James brightly.

'Yes. Taught them to lie still in the heather. That's about all I could do.'

'I read the season is rotten,' said Andrew.

'So it is.' Tom shoved a key into the lock and went into the house. 'Wait till I draw the curtains,' he said. 'Don't want any snoopers seeing lights.' We heard him moving about and presently strike a match and we watched him light an oil lamp. 'I like to be private.'

'Scotland,' muttered Andrew.

'Had a word with the deer in the Highlands.' Tom raised the lamp so that its light shone on us. 'Do I understand we have visitors tonight?'

'All the partridges from the Broughton shoot,' I said. 'And Vice wants to bring the pheasants when their time comes.'

'Good, good.' Tom was looking at us wolfishly. 'They can spend their weekends here if they wish.'

'Where's Floss?' Joker was looking up at Tom and wagging his tail.

'Ah, Floss. She's on her way.' Joker and Blueprint turned back to meet her. 'Come upstairs,' said Tom.

We followed him up a rickety staircase.

'He behaves as though it was *his* house,' muttered James.

'It *is* my house,' said Tom. He lit another lamp and we stared in wonder. The walls of the passage were lined with bookshelves and as he led us from room to room we saw books everywhere. Tom drew shabby but beautiful curtains across the windows as he went and lit candles and we stared at old lovely furniture. Pictures hung on the walls, and on the mantelshelves and in the corner cupboards we saw gleaming glass and china and unpolished silver. Paper was scattered over a writing table.

'Then you are not a tramp?' James could pop out with the most embarrassing questions.

'Oh yes, in a way, but a scholar too.'

'I thought you just lay about,' said Angela.

'I do. I do. Now here, I think, come the dogs.' Tom cocked his head on one side and Vice retreated under the bed.

'No need to be afraid,' said Tom rather maliciously, greatly raising our spirits. 'I went to the Farne Islands, too, you see. I have a plan to redistribute the seals.'

Vice came out from under the bed, which was a dusty four-poster with velvet hangings, extremely faded. 'You smell delicious,' he said. 'Fishy. Seals, I suppose.'

The dogs came in. Floss jumped on to the bed, curled up, put her nose under her bushy tail. I could tell she wasn't sleeping because her ears were half-cocked.

'How did you get here?' asked Tom, who was rummaging in a cupboard. 'Can I offer you a drink?' he said courteously to Angela, and without waiting for an answer poured brandy into a small glass and handed it to her. He did the same for me and the boys and poured out a tumblerful for himself. 'Drink up,' he said, eyeing us with amusement. 'Put a match to the fire, Andrew, it's ready laid.'

Andrew lit the fire. Vice sat immediately in front of it, staring at the flames as they leapt from one dry twig to another and set the logs burning.

'Where is the car?' I asked.

'In the quarry,' said Tom. 'I came the rest of the way on foot.'

'An otter caught a salmon,' said Floss.

'Dear me,' said Tom, adding rather hungrily, 'any left?'

'Plenty,' said Floss loftily. 'It said it had forgotten.'

'Then show Blueprint where it is, there's a darling, and bring it here. We all forget sometimes.' Floss got up and went out with Blueprint.

'What's the idea?' Andrew looked at Tom, who was looking at the flames of the fire through his glass, squinting down his long nose.

'The people who preserve the seals in the Farne Islands keep their numbers down, as they put it, by killing off a certain number every year.'

'I've read about it,' I said.

'We all have,' said James. 'It's disgusting.'

'Well, I thought so too, and as I was up that way I called.'

'Warning the grouse and the deer,' said Andrew.

'Yes, yes. I did that. It will cost a lot of money.' Tom gulped some brandy and laughed.

'Who to?' I said.

'All the people who have rented grouse moors and deer forests.'

'Good,' said Angela.

'And the seals?' Andrew returned to the point.

'Ah, yes, the seals. There is the north Devon coast, very rough and nasty. Quite a number of places in Cornwall. South-West Ireland, of course, and the coasts of Scotland. A lot of excellent places. Wales too. I shall tell them.'

'How wonderful that would be.' Angela's face was glowing.

'Yes.' Tom was sitting in a wing chair by the fire. 'Go and give the dogs a hand, boys.' Below us we could hear Floss being very governessy to Blueprint. The boys went out and presently came back carrying half a fish. They looked astonished and shamefaced.

'Surely not *our* otters!' I exclaimed.

'Well, it's dead now. We might as well eat it.' Tom pulled a sharp knife from his pocket and sliced the fish into steaks and impaled each steak with a stick. 'Grill 'em. They're delicious. I'm no saint. Nor are they.'

We grilled the steaks in silence and ate them pensively, pretending not to enjoy them.

'Father is looking for you to help with the farm,' said Andrew.

'Is he?' said Tom. 'Could do with some money. It was an expensive trip. Petrol and oil and so on.'

'Our father gave all the money he was paid for the fishing to the R.S.P.C.A.,' said Angela suddenly. 'We could have used it.' Tom nodded.

Floss looked at us and said in a nasty whining voice: 'Isn't it time you left? We are tired.'

We all stood up and said goodbye to Tom.

'What about the partridges?' I asked Vice.

'I'll lead them back.' Vice rose, arching his back.

We left the house with Blueprint and Joker and stood in a group in the moonlight, looking at the dark house behind us. A soft rustle came from behind the house. Round the corner came Vice, followed by a seemingly endless procession of partridges. 'It's not far as the crow flies,' said Blueprint.

'I think Vice is very clever,' I said.

'He frightened us,' said Andrew resentfully.

'Usually Tom gets a fox to cry out if anyone gets near here. Floss told me.' Joker stood by us waiting and listening.

'Time we went home,' James exclaimed and we hurried away. We reached home and our mother said: 'Where on earth have you been?' when we arrived.

'We were looking for a nightjar,' I said easily.

'There are no nightjars round here. They prefer sandy soil.' Get our mother on to birds and you are safe. 'Time you were in bed,' she said.

We hurried to bed and put out our lights. In the dark Angela came into my room. 'There's something funny about Tom Foley,' she whispered. 'Did you see all those books?'

'Yes.'

'That house, that car, his way of life.'

'It seems a nice way of life,' I said. 'Independent.'

'He drinks,' said Angela.

'So does the Master's horse when he gets the chance,' I said. 'He likes beer.'

'Get some sleep and don't disturb other people.' Mr Bull fidgeted in his cage. I could hear him fluffing up his feathers. The mouse climbed up on to my bed for a bit of conversation.

'Vice frightened us,' I whispered to the mouse.

The mouse tittered. 'He frightens us too.'

15

The following day I woke to Mr Bull's piping. Angela was still asleep and Blueprint and Vice lay on her bed in attitudes of deep repose. I wondered how and when Vice had got in.

My parents were breakfasting in the kitchen. I joined them. The telephone rang and my mother answered it. She listened.

'I'll see whether he is still here,' she said. My father turned the paper over and drank some coffee.

'I'm not here,' he said, gripping the paper. My father grinned and winked at me. 'White lies – useful.' He laid the paper on one side and helped himself to more coffee.

'Oh, how very interesting,' said my mother into the telephone. 'No,' she said firmly, 'I've no idea when he will be back. Why don't you ring him up tomorrow from London?' We heard her put the receiver back.

'Honestly,' said my mother, coming back into the room. 'Such a bad example for the children.'

'I won't be bothered on Sundays,' said my father, begging the question. 'Bad for my ulcers. Who was it?'

'That man who runs the Syndicate. He says their keepers tell them the Broughton place is alive with partridges, and there wasn't a bird there yesterday.'

'They can't shoot on Sunday,' said my father.

'That's why they are so cross,' said my mother.

'Hah!' My father laid his coffee cup back in the saucer and stood up, holding the paper. 'Useful clients. Top fees.'

'You are a disgrace,' said my mother amiably.

'Must educate the girls.' My father left the room.

'Living at home is an education in itself,' I said.

'I wonder what you mean by that?' My mother began clearing the breakfast things. I helped her.

'Who collects for the R.S.P.C.A. here?' I asked.

'The Master of the Hounds and the wife of the man who has the otter hounds,' said my mother in a flat voice. 'And,' she said, her voice rising, 'neither of them approves of stag hunting.'

'Surprise, surprise,' I said.

My mother began washing up. I went upstairs and woke Angela, who yawned and groaned.

'Let me out into the garden.' Blueprint trotted to the door. I let him out and went back to Angela.

'Stag hunting,' I said.

'Oh! I'd forgotten it. Will you and James find Tom?'

'All right,' I said. 'What do we say to him?'

'Tell him stag hunting is starting. He will think of something.'

I went down to the Johnsons' and found James. 'We've got to find Tom,' I said. 'He can send the pigeons.'

'Andrew is going to help my father.'

'What's he doing?'

'Rounding up sheep.'

'On a Sunday?'

'The sheep don't know it's Sunday.'

We went straight into the wood, skirted its edge to keep out of sight and walked, as we had walked the night before, to the hidden house. There was a slight misting rain and the trees dripped on us. We met a fox who said over its shoulder as it trotted into the wood: 'The keepers aren't half mad.'

'What are they doing?' James asked.

'Grumbling. They got no tips!'

When we reached the clearing we stopped and looked across at the house.

'No smoke,' said James. We walked round the clearing and tried the back door, which was not locked.

'He was tired last night,' I said.

'All the same we must tell him.' James held out a hand to me.

'Floss?' James called gently and enquiringly. There was no answer.

'Let's go up.' I followed him up the rickety stairs. He pushed open the door and again we listened. Outside the water was dripping from the gutters and pattering on the windows. We went into the room we had been in the night before. There was nobody. No Tom. No Floss.

'All gone,' said James and went across to the fireplace. 'The ashes are cold,' he whispered.

'We could lay his fire for him,' I said.

We took sticks from a big pile near the hearth and laid logs on them.

'Let's look round. We only saw it in the dark.' James was incurably curious. We looked round the room at the dusty bed and furniture, the books and china and the silver and the huge bed. We went into other rooms but there was nobody there. We went back to the room we had all sat in the night before.

'It's fishy, I mean it smells fishy,' said James.

'And of drink,' I said. 'Personally, I believe it's haunted,' I added, staring at a dirty old typewriter on the desk. 'What does he want this for?'

'I swear it's haunted,' said James. 'But only by Tom.'

'There's nobody here anyway,' I said.

We walked thoughtfully down into the village. From the pub we could hear a lot of talk and a good deal of laughter. As we passed the hotel we noticed that all the smart cars belonging to the shooting people had gone and only the Mr Cardigans' car was in the garage. One of the brothers was sitting in the garden reading. He waved to us and we went up to him.

'No fishing today,' he said. It was the older, fatter Mr Cardigan. 'It's Sunday.'

'Yes,' said James. 'You can't fish on Sunday.'

'Whether it's Sunday or any other day of the week, we still don't catch any fish.'

'You've been very nice about it,' I said.

'We've enjoyed ourselves. We still are enjoying ourselves. Not like those people who came down to shoot.'

'Didn't they enjoy themselves?' James sat down beside Mr Cardigan.

'No,' said Mr Cardigan, 'they did not. They expected a

lot of dead birds and they got none. We expect a lot of dead fish and get none. But we love watching the birds and animals. There's a difference.'

'My mother and James's mother watch birds,' I said.

'So do cats,' said Mr Cardigan. 'We've watched fish, too. There are plenty of fish in that water. It's very clear. It's a very odd thing.' Mr Cardigan gazed into the distance. 'The forty pounds arrived back by post.'

'How very odd,' I said.

'Yes. Local postmark too. Have a sweet.' Mr Cardigan offered a bag of peppermints. We said thank you and both blushed as we said goodbye. Mr Cardigan's face was expressionless.

'Even if he did know he wouldn't tell,' I said.

We walked on past the pub. On the step sat Joker.

'Father must be in there,' said James.

'He is,' said Joker. 'And Floss,' he added.

'Is Tom there?'

'Yes, he's hearing how there were no partridges to shoot.'

'Is that why they are laughing?'

'Yes.' Joker laid his nose on his paws and closed his eyes.

'Will you tell Floss we want to see Tom?'

'I might.' We knew from Joker's voice that he had been told to wait outside and was put out about it.

'Please, Joker.'

At that moment Mr Johnson, Tom and Floss came out of the pub. They all looked very cheerful.

'Hullo, you two,' said Mr Johnson.

'Hullo,' we said.

Mr Johnson and Joker got into his Landrover and drove off.

'What do you want?' said Tom. 'I'm busy.'

'Tom, the stag hunting has begun. Can you send your pigeons?'

'Easily,' said Tom good-humouredly. 'What do I do with the deer?'

'Oh, Floss can talk to the hounds and will you tell the deer to take to the forests?'

'Got to get them started.'

'You ask our mothers,' I said. 'They hate stag hunting.'

'Me?' Tom looked horrified. 'How could they help?'

'Money,' I said. 'They'll buy maize for your birds.'

'They think I'm a layabout in fact. It's better not to tell them.'

'You were at school with that awful man who was rude to mother at the Meet,' I said smugly.

'Blast you,' said Tom.

'We'll tell them you own the secret house.' James danced out of Tom's reach.

'Don't you dare!' Tom was furious. 'It's private.'

'We will,' I said, as Floss nipped me.

'Now, Floss.' Tom looked at the blood flowing freely from my calf and handed me a dirty handkerchief which I tied round my leg. James ignored my wound and pressed on with our advantage.

'I'll see.' Tom looked at James grumpily and added: 'It's blackmail.'

'What's blackmail?' The younger Mr Cardigan approached us from behind. Floss growled.

'Oh, the children are trying to blackmail me into protesting about stag hunting.'

'Stag hunting is disgusting,' said the younger Mr Cardigan.

'You are a fisherman,' Tom said rather rudely.

'Well, I fish, but the fish have choice. Hunting is quite different. However, there's always the hope that the people will break their necks,' said Mr Cardigan, smiling at his brother.

'Angela hunts,' I said.

'I understand there's every hope she will break her neck,' said Tom nastily. 'You are very Jesuitical.'

'Tell you what, Foley,' said the younger Mr Cardigan suddenly. 'You drive over and protest. Interrupt them.'

'Splendid idea, splendid,' said Tom acidly.

'Just exactly my idea of fun,' said Floss, standing up against Tom, wagging her bushy tail.

'What is Jesuitical?' I muttered, not wishing to show my ignorance. James shrugged his shoulders, equally baffled.

'They seem to know each other.' Blueprint, who had been shocked by Floss's behaviour, looked mystified.

❧ 16 ❧

After lunch that Sunday the four of us walked up to the quarry and Andrew and James lifted the cover off Tom Foley's car and gave it a good look.

'It's in marvellous condition for its age.' Andrew stroked the old paintwork.

'He doesn't use it much.' James stood on the running-board and peered inside before Andrew replaced the groundsheet reverently like a person covering a corpse he had just identified in a morgue.

'Is he really a tramp?' James looked at the sheeted car.

'I think so. Our father defended him last time he was had up for being drunk,' I said. 'He gets angry about things.'

'That doesn't make him a tramp,' Andrew said. 'And my father paid his fine.'

'I never knew that,' I said.

'Well, he helps father a lot on the farm. Father likes him.'

'Our fathers seem more human than we think,' said Angela. 'What about the poaching?'

'Perhaps he was hungry,' I said romantically.

'Don't be silly. He enjoys it,' Andrew said crushingly.

'He can't be a tramp if he owns a vintage car and a house,' James muttered. 'He knows the Cardigans.'

'He certainly looks like a tramp in that old hat of father's,' Andrew said.

'And the vicar's suit,' added Angela.

'He lives out.' Andrew tossed his head towards the badgers' sets. 'Sometimes.'

'Probably likes it,' said James. 'I would. No one to bother me. Why does he help us?'

'It amuses him, of course,' said Angela. 'Just as it amuses Marge and me to go hunting.'

'Oh,' we all said, heavily sarcastic, 'it *amuses* him.'

'There's more to it than that, of course.' Angela shifted from one foot to another.

'What?' I asked.

'I don't know,' said Angela. 'But just look what an inspiration he had about the foxes.'

'That was sheer genius,' said Andrew. 'Come on, we can't stop here.'

In the clearing Tom lay with Floss against him keeping a watchful eye open. She pricked her ears when we arrived and sat up.

'Are you asleep, Tom?' James asked respectfully.

'I was until I heard you all tramping up the hill.'

'We made no noise,' Angela said indignantly.

'My ears are close to the ground.'

'Sorry,' said Angela.

There was a long pause during which we sat in a row with Blueprint and looked down on Tom and Floss.

'Want to make plans about those deer, I suppose.' Tom spoke at last. 'The Cardigans will be amused.'

'Oh,' said Angela. 'So the Cardigans are with us?'

'In spirit, yes. I've sent the pigeons.'

'That will help,' I said politely.

'It isn't until Saturday. Can't you let me sleep?'

We felt dismissed.

'Do you really do nothing?' asked James, Floss sneered.

'As little as one can in this Welfare State.'

'You own a car and a house,' James said.

'I scribble.' Tom's voice repressed laughter.

'We are taught to write clear script,' James said. 'Some people learn Italic.'

'Really. How is the leg?' Tom addressed me.

'I shan't get blood poisoning,' I said tartly, feeling that we were all being made fun of.

'Time you left me in peace,' Tom said rudely.

We got up without speaking and went away to the Johnsons'.

'Do you like sheep?' Angela said to Mrs Johnson.

'Of course I do,' said Mrs Johnson. 'Earwigs are good mothers too.'

'What does she mean, earwigs?' I asked Angela as we walked home.

'She means earwigs and sheep are good mothers.'

'Then why doesn't she say so?'

'She's grown-up.' Angela gave a childish skip. 'I must go and talk to Marge.'

'Why Marge?' I found Angela very aggravating.

'Well, Mr Bodkin is going to keep her as a brood mare. She's engaged to a thoroughbred.'

'Heaven help him,' said Blueprint, who didn't like that word.

'How is the Pony Club?' I asked hurriedly.

'Never been better,' said Angela sweetly. 'They are much more confident.'

'Since they had rides on Marge, I suppose,' said Blueprint.

'That's about it.' Angela ran off.

'And none of them has seen a fox cub killed,' I said to Blueprint as we went home.

'Who bit your leg?' said my mother.

'It's just a scratch. I'll put a plaster on it.' I went up to Mr Bull.

'Don't you feel frustrated, Mr Bull, with all the birds getting ready to migrate?'

'Thankful I'm not,' said Mr Bull. 'No place like home.'

'Even bullfinches spout platitudes.' The mouse was peering out of its hole.

'You eat his spare seed, don't insult him.' I said.

The mouse sat up and began washing itself. 'I hear quite a lot is planned for Saturday,' it said, brushing its whiskers forward with its paws.

I looked at the mouse suspiciously, but it was squinting down its nose like Tom Foley. 'What do you know about Saturday?' I said. The mouse whisked back down its hole without answering. I went out to visit Gertrude.

Gertrude was lying on her side, keeping one eye on her porkers, who were rooting and playing round the field.

'Gertrude,' I said, 'do you know what is going on?'

'Yes,' Gertrude grunted without moving.

'Mr Bull and the mouse know something too.'

'Anything may happen.' Gertrude was enigmatic.

'Gertrude, you are a pig,' I said.

'True.' Gertrude's side heaved with laughter. I went away and sat in the sunlight until I saw our mother walking up through the wood with Andrew.

'Hullo,' she said. 'Andrew says you got bitten, not scratched. All you children are such ready liars. Your father says it will stand you in very good stead in later life.'

'How cynical,' said James, joining us from the farm.

'Lawyers have to be.' My mother smiled. 'It's not exactly included in law exams but they learn it. Andrew has been buying maize. I gave him an advance.'

James and I looked innocently at my mother, and Blueprint gazed ahead of him, his tail curled round his feet and his long ears drooping.

'Ah, here come the Cardigans.' My mother looked at the two brothers, each carrying a rod and creel, walking towards us. 'Come and have a cup of tea and tell us about the fishing,' she said to them. The Cardigans hesitated, then followed us to the house.

Angela got back a little later from cubbing. The Master stopped his horse-box near our house and let down the ramp. Angela led Marge down into the lane.

'Had a good day?' I asked.

'Lost the whole pack. I've left the Whip to look for them.' The Master sounded angry. 'I shall sue those people,' he said.

'What for?' I asked.

'I'll get your father to think of something.'

Angela grinned and helped the Master shut the back of his horse-box. 'Thank you for a lovely day,' she said.

The Master drove off waving goodbye. Marge lowered her head and blew down her nose at Vice, who recoiled and spat. 'Now then, Marge,' said Angela. But Marge suddenly darted away down the lane with the reins dangling and her head nodding high in the air.

'She overdoes it,' said Angela.

'She will stop when she gets to Bodkin's field,' said Vice.

'I know.' Angela went after Marge.

'I wonder what her foal will be like when she has one,' I said.

'Not a patch on its mother. Marge is a natural.' Blueprint shifted his weight against my legs.

Mr Bull was sitting in his cage by the open window listening to the birds singing and chattering outside, and I sat beside him watching the swallows and martins wheel and soar. Several pigeons flew past and into the wood.

'What's happening?' I asked Mr Bull.

Mr Bull hopped a little closer to the window. 'Let me out,' he said. I let him out and watched him flip his wings and swoop down and disappear into the hedge between our garden and the road.

'Leave the cage door open. He's gathering news.' The mouse was looking out of its hole and all I could see was whiskers and bright eyes.

'Come out,' I said to the mouse.

'No thanks.' The mouse stayed where it was. 'There's a lot going to happen,' it said.

'Rubbish,' I said uneasily. 'Floss will lead the deer to safety and Tom will be there.'

'When?' asked the mouse, peeping out of its hole.

'There is going to be plenty of trouble for the Syndicate because our constable is on to the traps. Tom said to meet him tonight,' I said. 'I suppose Floss will lead the deer to the sets.'

'No she won't.' The mouse poked its nose slightly further from the hole so that I could see the pink transparency of its ears.

'I've word from the pigeons,' Mr Bull piped as he came back. 'The deer have gone to the house – Tom's house.'

'What's going on?' Angela said idly as she came in.

'Evacuation,' Mr Bull answered at once. 'And they are making up a party in the next village to go badger baiting at dawn, and Floss will have all the deer at Tom's place.'

'They can't dig badgers!' I exclaimed.

'They can,' said the mouse.

'But nobody ever goes there.' Angela looked put out. 'It's secret. It's a Nature Reserve.'

'Quick, Mr Bull, send a message to Tom,' I said.

'The pigeons have gone. It's all right.'

'Blueprint,' I said urgently, 'can you go and tell Floss. It's Floss the badgers trust. We must tell her. I'm going to find Andrew,' and I went downstairs with Blueprint, who trotted away towards the woods and the badgers. I ran through the wood to the pig field.

'Gertrude,' I called. Gertrude grunted. 'Gertrude, you have brains. We hear there is a party on to bait badgers.'

'Ah,' said Gertrude. 'Leave it to Tom. Tell Andrew.' She closed her eyes and lay where she was, a huge mass of pink pig.

'Gertrude!' I said. Gertrude heaved a sigh.

After a long search I found Andrew sitting by the river with Joker. I told him about the badger baiting and he went quite white with rage. Joker licked his face.

'Oh!' Andrew cried out. 'Does Gertrude know?'

'I told her but she just lies there doing nothing.'

'She's thinking,' said Andrew defensively.

'Looks more like sleeping to me,' I said. 'Blueprint has gone to tell the badgers. So have the pigeons.'

'Good,' said Andrew. 'Floss will help. What time are they going to do it?' Andrew appeared to be keeping his head.

'At dawn,' said a voice behind us. We turned round and saw that we were being observed by a sheep.

'How do you know?' Joker asked arrogantly.

'The postman's dog told me this morning before you were up. It's a dirty business.' The sheep wandered away nibbling at the short grass as it went. 'It's supposed to be very sporting.'

'Hullo,' said the Cardigans as they passed us. 'Very peaceful, isn't it?'

'Yes,' I said.

'Back to the hurly-burly of city life next week,' the elder Mr Cardigan remarked.

'We shall miss the peace and quiet,' said the other.

'Really?' said Andrew.

'Earning one's living is a cut-throat business,' said the younger Mr Cardigan. 'You children wouldn't believe what city life is like after the charms of the country.'

'Don't forget we have to meet Tom tonight,' said Andrew. 'We must go there with Joker and Blueprint anyway. Let's all meet when our parents have gone to bed and go up to Tom's house.' Andrew was watching the Cardigans walking up the river. 'Cut-throat business indeed.'

'No use fussing,' said Joker. 'I want my dinner.'

I left Andrew and took the short cut home through the pig field. As I passed Gertrude's little corrugated covered house I said goodbye curtly. Gertrude still lay on her side but her tiny brown eye with a flash of red in it caught mine. 'Go away. I'm thinking,' she said. 'Tom is a poet.' I remembered the dusty typewriter and laughed.

At home the telephone was ringing as I went to wash my hands. 'I'm in,' said my father and went to the telephone and said, 'Jones here'. There was a long crackle in the telephone and my father listened. Finally he said: 'Very well, I'll see about it tomorrow. By the way, did you know your keepers have been using traps? Illegal, you know. You will be summoned for that. Heavy fines.' He put down the receiver and smiled.

'What does he want?' asked my mother.

'He wants retribution of some kind,' said my father.

'It's queer,' said my mother. 'The place is alive with game.'

'Traps too,' said my father as we went in to supper.

'Expensive litigation?' I asked.

'Oh, yes.' My father accepted a bowl of soup from my mother.

'What about the traps?' said Angela who had come in.

'They will be fined,' said my father. 'Against the law now.'

'I hope they get fined a lot,' said Angela.

'I expect they will,' said my father. 'The Master of Foxhounds is on the bench.'

The telephone rang again and my father answered it. There was a long roar down the instrument and my father listened with an expression of growing amusement.

'Well, well,' he said. 'It's not illegal, old boy. Somebody being funny, I expect.'

'Not on speaking terms,' we heard from where we sat. My father came back to the table and finished eating his soup. 'It appears there was some sort of mix-up with the shoot and the hounds.'

We told him and he laughed again.

'It's curious that you and the Johnson boys were all there,' he said.

'What do you mean, curious?' said Angela.

'I mean what I say,' said my father, giving Blueprint a small bit of cheese.

My mother looked out across the garden. 'I do wish Vice would leave the birds in peace,' she said.

'I expect he is just curious,' I said.

'What time shall we go?' I asked Angela as we went to bed.

'One o'clock should do.' Angela got into bed with Blueprint.

'Can you wake me at half-past twelve?' I said to the mouse.

'All right,' said the mouse, taking the bit of cheese I had brought for it. 'Where is Vice?'

'Gone out,' I said. 'Who is doing this badger baiting?'

'I'll find out,' said the mouse, and took the cheese into its hole.

'Will he?' I asked Mr Bull as I gave him fresh water.

'Yes, he will ask his cousins in the garden.'

'Will they know?'

'Well, mice are a gossipy lot.'

I went to bed and slept until the mouse woke me up by walking over my face. I sneezed and went and woke Angela. We dressed and crept downstairs with Blueprint and went out of the house. 'Party from the next village baiting,' squeaked the mouse.

Vice joined us, and as quickly as we could we walked

down to the Johnsons' bridge. Andrew and James were waiting for us with Joker. None of us said anything as we set off through the wood towards Tom's house.

An owl hooted twice in the wood and the two dogs stopped and listened.

'Fancy that,' said Vice.

'What did he say?' asked Andrew.

'Good luck and goodbye. Queer.'

We made our way to the hidden clearing. The house was grey, dark and silent, showing no sign of life. Vice led the way, on silent paws, followed rather furtively by the dogs.

'Come on,' said Andrew. But we all stood stock still and I reached for Angela's hand. Shapes were dotted about the clearing, shapes which disappeared silently into the wood or stood staring at us with great eyes.

'Deer,' said Andrew, letting out his breath with a sigh. 'It's the deer.'

'Only some of them.' Tom had come to the door of the house and stood in the darkness watching us.

'Oh, Tom!' James's voice was full of relief. 'Oh, Tom!'

'I've distributed the greater part of the deer among the Forestry lands. Only the larger stags are here.'

'What about the badgers?' James asked.

'They will be here presently.'

'How lovely,' said Andrew.

'Empty sets.' Tom chuckled.

'I asked the mouse to find out who they were,' I said.

'I know,' said Blueprint. 'Three men from the further village, the postman and the boy from the garage.'

'Five,' I said. 'They will get cold waiting.'

'Come in.' Tom led the way into the house. He lit no lamp

and everything looked strange in the moonlight. We kept close together. 'We must wait for the badgers.' Tom led us into the strange room with the big bed in it. He lay down on the bed and we all sat on the floor with Joker, Blueprint and Vice.

'It's promising, very promising.' Tom laughed an almost silent laugh. 'In fact, when people go to kill their fellow creatures they may get quite worried. Seals are highly intelligent. And Vice's idea about the partridges and pheasants is already catching on all over the country.'

'That's wonderful,' I said.

'The foxes and hounds have got organised as well,' Tom murmured. 'Of course there will be casualties, as no one can stop the fox's natural habits, any more than ours.'

'But hunting is going to get a boost,' said Angela. 'Hounds, horses and people are going to enjoy themselves tremendously.'

'Yes, I think they will,' said Tom.

'The Emperor has no clothes,' I said.

'Yes, but who is going to point that out? No one.'

'The otters, in spite of being so unsociable, are spreading the news as well, and the deer have undertaken to move off the moors every hunting day.'

'How will they know when it's a hunting day?' said James.

'We will send news by the birds.'

'Here comes Floss.' Joker spoke with his ears pricked and nose up.

We went to the window and looked out. Floss trotted into the clearing, her tail carried high and bushy, her pointed ears pricked and her bright white and brown markings showing clear in the moonlight. Behind her seemed to drift shadows which we only recognised as badgers when they ambled through a shaft of moonshine which showed up their heavily marked faces. We left the house and Floss came up to Tom, wagging her tail and her whole hind quarters, her ears lowered and her bared teeth grinning in the moonlight. Tom picked her up and held her against his chest while she licked his face.

'My darling,' said Tom.

'The keepers are joining in the badger dig.' Floss spoke in her usual whining voice.

'Are they indeed?'

'All the men are gathered about three, so that they can be at the sets at dawn.' A badger spoke from among the trees.

Tom stood thinking, and then we heard him murmur: 'Four children, three dogs, one cat and one man.' Floss, still in Tom's arms, put her nose up to his ear. Tom listened and laughed. 'Come on,' he said. 'Out into the clearing.'

We gathered in a group round Tom, who stood with Floss in his arms, looking round him. I could feel the ground cold under my feet and looked up at the moon. All round us we could see deer with their nervous ears cocked, watching with wide eyes. The badgers walked ponderously but silently up to Tom, paying no attention to us.

'They are short-sighted, almost blind.' Tom felt in his pockets for scraps which he gave them.

Several foxes began playing in the moonlight and Joker and Blueprint peered at them eagerly, then suddenly, as though unleashed, made a dash in pursuit and the foxes and dogs careered away in a hunt through the wood.

'No!' I exclaimed. 'They can't.'

'It is their nature so to do.' Tom quoted some poet we had never read. 'They won't catch them and they will go home. Listen.'

We heard the crashing approach of a large animal and presently Gertrude came waddling into the clearing and walked up to Tom, pushing her way through the other animals until she rubbed herself against Tom's legs. Tom, holding Floss, whose ears were pricked towards the distant hunt after the foxes, bent down and listened to something Gertrude was saying to him.

'Very well.' Tom smiled ruefully. Gertrude turned and left the clearing as noisily as she had come. As she went, the deer and badgers disappeared silently among the trees.

'Gertrude always knows best.' Tom stroked Floss, who licked his face. 'Gertrude is a thinker. Time you all went home, isn't it?'

We felt dismissed and, saying a subdued goodnight, we left the clearing as Tom went into his house with Floss, shutting the door behind him.

'The dogs behaved outrageously,' Angela said angrily.

'Quite naturally and harmlessly.' Andrew tossed the sentence over his shoulder rather crushingly.

When we reached the Johnsons' farm Joker barked and came bounding out to meet the boys, leaping up at them and wagging his tail.

'Where have you been?' Mr Johnson called to them. 'Give Joker a rub down, Andrew, he's been out hunting.'

'Sheep?' asked James in a voice which verged on the impertinent.

'Of course not. A fox, I expect, coming over our land. No harm done,' Mr Johnson's cheerful voice answered.

Angela and I cut across the pig field towards our house and as we passed Gertrude's hut I flashed my torch, catching her tiny red eye which gleamed like a ruby. 'You are a fraud,' I said to her. Gertrude grunted sleepily.

'Silence is golden,' she said.

'Nobody could call you silent,' Angela said from behind me.

'There's silence and speech.' Gertrude did not bother to move. 'We get on very well without your kind of speech.'

'But you understand us,' I said.

'Oh yes, but it's better to leave you guessing. We've decided.'

'Cheek,' said Angela, pulling me away. 'Absolute cheek. They are going to leave us out again.'

'It will save them a lot of trouble,' I said as we hurried home along the river path.

'It was a sort of ultimatum she made.' Angela was resentful. 'Do you suppose it will apply to them all?'

'We'll soon see,' I said and then stopped dead and pointed.

In a deep pool the otters were playing, the young ones chasing each other through the water and up on to rocks with incredible agility. On the bank their parents watched, making an occasional dive, tweaking one of their offspring under water. We stood watching entranced until the father otter reared himself up on his hind legs on the bank and stared at us. There was just enough light to see his bright beady eyes and twitching whiskers. He gave us a long appraising look then made a signal and slid silently into the water. There were one or two unusual swirls and eddies and then no noise except the noise of the river.

When we reached home my mother exclaimed: 'Really, girls, you must not stay out so late!'

'There is always a first time,' said my father, who stood at the top of the stairs in his pyjamas.

'And a last.' Angela took the full brunt of Blueprint's greeting as he hurled himself on to her chest and, overbalancing, sat down.

'Go to bed,' said my mother.

Upstairs, as Angela and Blueprint got into bed, I watched the mouse scuttle away into the hole by the electric light socket. I took the cover off Mr Bull's cage and gave him some hempseed which he took from between my fingers and crushed between his strong snippers.

'You started all this,' I said, looking into his large brown eyes. 'We shall always know that you can speak if you want to: that you can all of you speak but won't: that you can all understand us but we can't understand you. I suppose you are afraid of getting vulgarised and put on the movies? I suppose you want to keep the upper hand?'

Mr Bull did not answer but closed his eyes, pulling up one sticklike leg among his stomach feathers.

I put the cover back on his cage and got into bed with Vice, who was paying me an unusual visit as he normally preferred to sleep with Angela.

'Budge up,' I said to Vice, who was curled into a tight ball in the middle of the bed. 'You heard me.'

Vice yawned and stretched out a long foreleg, pricking me through the blankets with his claws. I laughed and made myself as comfortable as I could, listening sleepily to Vice purring and later having small dreams in which he made tiny mewing noises.

❧ 18 ❧

'Oh, do look!' exclaimed my mother at breakfast as she read the paper. 'Poems by Thomas Foley to be published by Cardigan and Cardigan. Can they be ours?'

'Yes. Couple of intellectuals,' said my father, plunging his knife into the marmalade. 'Poetry never makes money. I do though.'

'Litigation?' enquired my mother.

'Yes.' My father looked rather pleased with himself. 'The Cardigans have a sense of humour though.' He opened one of his letters and read it while we all watched him, especially Blueprint who was hoping for some scraps. 'They have reserved the fishing for next year and sent a cheque. Rather a nice way to put us at our ease since they caught no fish. They say it is to preserve the river for the otters.'

'There are no otters,' said my mother mechanically.

'No,' said my father, 'maybe not. Johnson says there are none.'

'Is Thomas Foley Tom Foley?' I asked.

'Of course. Didn't you know?' My father laughed and Angela and I looked at each other in outraged surprise.

'Another thing none of you know, as you were watching television' – my father grinned at my mother – 'and you girls were out doing God knows what, is that there was quite a battle last night in the village pub. The police were called in.'

'What about?' I asked.

'Well, I was having a quiet drink with Johnson and the Cardigans to say goodbye to them when a row blew up between the gamekeepers and the Huntsman and Whip. They started abusing each other because each thinks the other is to blame because there are no foxes or partridges about this year. They came to blows. Quite a battle.'

'I wish I had been with you,' said my mother. 'I am handy with an umbrella.'

'Johnson and the landlord put them all out in the street and they fought there.' My father answered Blueprint's gaze and gave him a rind of bacon. 'It wasn't fun,' my father went on. 'Several people got hurt. I never like to see people like that; it was ugly. Luckily the police came along. We shall have quite a case on our hands.'

'I thought you hated notoriety,' said my mother. 'You will get it, as the Master of Hounds is on the Bench and so is the Master of Otter Hounds.'

'I think it may go further than that. He's giving up otter hunting and like all converts is swinging the other way. He wants the protection of *all* Wild Life. We will get the girls educated yet. If I know these chaps we'll have a High Court case. Reporters prowling round and so on.'

'Oh, they will disturb the birds!' my mother cried angrily.

I went upstairs and put Mr Bull's cage by my window and sat down and told him the news my father had brought.

'Now you broadcast it,' I said when I had finished telling him and gave him some hempseed. Without haste Mr Bull crunched the seed and then, puffing himself up, began to pipe loudly, and in the garden, though the nesting season was long over, the birds answered him in chorus.

'What's he on about?' Angela came into the room with Blueprint.

'At a guess I should say he is telling them we are worse than they are,' I said. 'But from now on we must guess what's going on and tell them, mustn't we?'

'Floss will laugh,' said Angela, 'and Marge.'